A World of Difference

By the same author:

A WORLD OF DIFFERENCE

by Bentz Plagemann

William Morrow and Company, Inc.

NEW YORK 1969

TO **D.W.M.**
and the future

A World of Difference

CHAPTER ONE

THE first time we met the Baileys we had no idea of what they would come to mean to us, and how, in time, they would even change our lives, or at least our attitude toward life. I think we even resented them a little at first when they moved into the empty house next door. We had been alone in our old house in the country, Kate and I, trying to resolve a dilemma which I suppose most people must face at a certain time in their lives. Our son had left us. He had taken his wife and his infant son and had gone away. Of course he hadn't left us just to get away from us, or at least we hoped that wasn't the reason. He had a new job which had called him to another part of the country, and we had a feeling, the world being what it is today, that from now on it was going to be that way. It seemed unlikely that circumstances would ever bring Cam and Nancy and little John back to live in our village again.

It was as if a planet had broken away from a galaxy in which it had circled for so long, to set up a new planetary galaxy in another part of the firmament, and wasn't that the way it was supposed to be? Except that here we were, still in

13

our old orbit, still circling about in a galaxy from which a principal star had vanished. The celestial music seemed off key.

And now, as if to compound our sense of loss and change, there would be new people next door where the Harmons used to live. "Who has bought the Harmon house?" was the way I put it when I went to the post office on the day the For Sale sign was taken down. It would always be the Harmon house to us. Or so we thought then. We had loved the Harmons. We had been close to them all the years they had lived there. Kate and Nelly Harmon had made little tea parties for each other in the afternoon when their daily tasks were finished. They took turns, and if it wasn't Kate I saw from my upstairs study window, going across the lawn with something in her hand, a plate of freshly made cookies under a napkin, the slip of a begonia rooted in a water tumbler, a magazine with a new recipe, it would be Nelly coming up the walk to our porch, always with an air of suppressed excitement, for if Nelly did not carry some small gift in her hand, she brought, instead, the latest bulletin. It was Nelly who always knew who was going to have a baby, or who was going to marry whom, sometimes, it seemed, even before they knew it themselves, or who, alas, had just been taken to the hospital.

When Nelly died poor Clem Harmon was lost. He just didn't seem to know what to do with himself. He thought he wanted to stay in the house. He didn't want to go to live with any of his married children. He was retired from his job in the city. But he had always had hobbies and interests. Surely he was a man with enough inner resources to make a life for himself, or at least to face it alone. It was painful to watch him. His married children came to see him on weekends, bringing the grandchildren, and for a while there would be a spurt of activity in the old house, but during the week it was sad. Clem had always liked to garden, and he would be outside early in the morning, but what he seemed to be doing now was retrenching instead of planting anew. He dug up the asparagus bed. He dug up the strawberry bed. They were too difficult to take care of, he said. He had to remember that he was getting older. It would be easier to take care of everything if he just put it all into lawn. And then in the afternoon we would see him at another ritual. He would have a fire going in the back, in the empty oil drum, pierced with holes, where trash was burned, and he would be standing there burning papers, sheaves of letters, picking out one now and again to read before he consigned it to the flames. You can't imagine how relieved everyone was when the Arnolds in the village entertained Mrs. Arnold's sister, a fine and cheerful widow. Mrs. Mercer swept Clem off his feet and carried him right away from his sorrow and his mourning of the past.

The house had been empty, up for sale, for some months. It was a pretty old house. It was what is known as a Victorian half-house, a definition which Nelly Harmon had to explain to me in the beginning. A Victorian half-house was built, presumably by a young family, with the intention and hope, not always realized, of eventual expansion and enlargement. The architects of the period had developed a design for such a house which had its own symmetry even in its half-state. These houses may be recognized by their essential characteristic of double front doors which stand at the far right of the verandah, intended someday, when the house was completed, to stand in the middle of the verandah. Beyond the front doors is a hallway from which a stairway curves to the second floor. To the left is the parlor, and in back of the parlor is the dining room. The kitchen is directly in back of the front hall, the bedrooms are above, and if and when the house is ever completed, a door to the right in the front hall will lead to an even grander parlor, with a library beyond that, and more bedrooms above.

The Harmon house had never been completed. It remained a Victorian half-house, and under Clem's scrupulous care, and with Nelly's taste and her love of the period, it had been a perfect house, a gem of a house, a little house one might expect to find dismantled and restored in a museum. There were curtains with over-drapes at the windows. There were hooked rugs on the polished wide-board floors. There were sofas and chairs upholstered in velvet, and period lamps wired for electricity, and family portraits on the walls. On glass shelves in the windows of the dining room Nelly had arranged her collection of colored glass bottles. On winter evenings a fire burned decorously behind the old cast-iron fender of the fireplace in the parlor, and there was always a pleasant scent in the house, as of verbena, or lavender, or lemon-oil furniture polish.

All that was gone now. Gone with the wind. Gone with the roses. The people who had bought the house were the Baileys, the postmaster told me. They were a young family with two small children, he said, but no one knew anything about them.

Troubles never come singly, as we all know, and probably the only thing that saves us in the end is our ignorance of the future. Half our troubles don't even begin as troubles. They may even seem like dreams about to come true, or vice versa. When I came back from the post office, Kate told me that Bert Thompson had tried to reach me, and wanted me to call him back. My heart sank.

Bert Thompson is a literary agent. There are those who say that he is the best, the toughest, the most knowing literary

16

agent in all of New York, and it is true that when you get off
the elevator at the floor where his office is, you can smell the
money from around the corner. I had always hoped that a
quantity of it would somehow find its way to me, so that I
might even have to carry it home in shopping bags. This
hadn't happened yet, but the dream lived on, and I still remembered how proud I was when Bert had agreed to take
me on. When he sent me a revised list of his clients with my
name there, I got out of bed later that night to look at it
again to see what distinguished company I shared. When I
was finally committed to his way of doing business I found it
very difficult to disagree with him in any way. Those dreams
come true, the shopping bags full of money were always just
ahead.

But now he was bugging me about a project which I really
did protest. I had written a novel which had attracted a little
more attention than other novels I had written, and the week
before Bert had called me into town to tell me that there was
dramatic interest in it, whatever that meant. My initial reaction to this news, when the meaning of it was explained to
me, was that if there was any dramatic interest in my novel,
then let someone else do something about it, for it didn't
mean that the interest taken in my novel was dramatic in itself, but that someone thought there was a play in it, and if
that was so then let them write the play, because I didn't
know anything at all about the theater or about playwriting,
and from what I had heard I didn't think I wanted to know
anything about it.

Bert wasn't willing to accept this. There was a play in the
novel, he said, and I could write it. I must write it. "My God,
man," he said. "Think of the money! There could be a quarter of a million dollars in it, or maybe more. You would be
fixed for life. You could write anything you wanted to after

17

that. All you have to do is go in and make a quick killing and get out!"

We were having luncheon at Armand's: cocktails, melon and prosciutto; writers, editors, agents; flowers, crystal chandeliers, and the fleet, soft feet of waiters. The smell of success in the air was more heady than the scent of the flowers. Bert was figuring on the little note pad he always carried in his inside breast pocket. If I let someone else adapt the novel for the stage, even if I worked with someone else as a collaborator, it would be too costly. It wouldn't be fair. I could do it myself.

In Armand's I always felt dazed and numb, like the family idiot recluse suddenly brought downstairs from his room in the attic, and if you equated that with a writer's study on the second floor back of an old house in the country, you could see that the comparison was apt. I couldn't follow Bert's figures. I wanted to shield my eyes and ears from the glitter and the noise. But who was I to say no to Bert Thompson, the best, the toughest, the most knowing literary agent in New York? I said that I would think it over. Bert said fine, he knew I would see it his way, and he would set up an appointment for us with the first name on the list of interested producers.

That was what the telephone call from Bert was about, and that was why my heart sank. On the following morning, as he told me when I called him back, we were to go to see the first name on the list, an actor-producer-director with the improbable name of Alton Tweed.

The day of assignation dawned bright and clear, and I went into town to meet Bert as arranged on a corner of lower Fifth Avenue, the expensive outer circle of Greenwich Village. I felt preposterously apprehensive, for no reason that I could define, except that for all of my professional life I had worked in that closed room alone, on the second floor back of an old house in the country. Also, the reports of disaster I had heard from friends who had been persuaded to take a chance in the theater did nothing to allay my fears. But Bert guided me along, like a timid virgin going to her first tryst, toward the small, restored, nineteenth-century coach house where Alton Tweed lived.

Alton Tweed was not at home. His representative or assistant, a shining young man with the gravity of an archangel, did not reveal why Mr. Tweed had been called away, but he did inform us that he had been definitely authorized to negotiate for the property.

This word confused me. Bert, ordinarily efficient beyond reproach, had unaccountably failed to explain to me, presuming, I suppose, that I knew, that a novel is a novel only until a producer looks at it, after which it becomes a property and glows softly in the dark. By the time I had grasped this, several formal exchanges had already taken place between Bert and the assistant to Mr. Tweed, much like the opening passages of a Greek tragedy, and the whole thing began to seem like a play at which I had arrived several moments after the curtain had gone up.

The house itself was like a stage setting. The tone was so solemn and sincere that it seemed vulgar even to breathe. The room in which we sat, done up in tones of eggplant, celadon and beige, was a decorator's triumph, and I wished I had not been so casual that morning in the half-hearted attempt I had made to polish my shoes. There was a brass chandelier, and there were hunting prints, and crystal ashtrays as big as soup bowls. There was also a butler who had come from the nearest casting agency, and in this atmosphere of doomlike elegance tea or spirits were offered. I asked for a whiskey, needing it.

Mr. Tweed, his assistant said, had already approached the staging of my novel with a brilliant and original idea. It could be done as a comic strip, with life-size cutout figures on moving tracks to supplement, presumably, the living actors. He was certain that I would be enchanted by the idea. I said nothing, being busy with my glass. Had I seen Mr. Tweed's production of *Never in This World?* I had, and since I had, surely I would remember the ingenious solution to the problem of the second act curtain? Mr. Tweed felt that a great part of success in the New York theater was to keep always before one a mental picture of the opening night audience. The opening night audience was frivolous, bored, overfed, sophisticated, and addled by cocktails. They had to be hit in the face with custard pies. There had been some trouble in making the author of *Never in This World* understand this, and Mr. Tweed had been forced to take him out in a small boat to the middle of a lake he owned in the White Mountains to make him see it that way. I knew also, from my own contacts in the underground, that the author in question had once during rehearsals of "Never In This World" chased Mr. Tweed up Broadway at two o'clock one morning with the avowed intention of killing him for what he had done to his script, but since discretion is the better part of valor, I was silent.

I finished my drink, in its glass of crystal etched with Napoleonic bees, and put the glass down. I stood up. Bert stood up. He looked at me, and then he spoke for us. "We will think it over," he said.

When we reached the street, I turned to Bert. "I don't think I can do it," I said. "Someone would have to write a script for me."

20

"Now, we've been all over that," Bert said, with the literary agent's measured patience, much as a horse trainer soothes a skittish colt. "You know you can do it yourself."

"That isn't what I mean," I said. "That world in there is so unreal that first someone would have to write a script for me in which I would be a writer writing a play before I could even begin. Someone would have to give me my lines, before I could write the lines for the play."

"Oh," Bert said, looking puzzled.

"Besides," I said, "the idea of being taken out in a small boat to the middle of a lake in the White Mountains by Mr. Tweed really makes me quite nervous."

Bert shrugged his shoulders and looked at his watch. "Okay," he said. "I'll set up a date to meet the next one on the list. I'll be in touch with you. After all, what have you got to lose?"

Nothing but my innocence, I thought, prophetically.

When I arrived home the Baileys were in the process of moving in next door. They were all there except Father Bailey, who was presumably at his place of business. Kate was out on the lawn between our two houses with a little family group, and when she saw me drive in the driveway she waved for me to join them. I put the car away and walked toward them across the lawn, having an opportunity to observe them in advance. There was Mrs. Bailey, Laura, and there was little Billy, and little Suzy, none of whose names I knew as yet, but as I approached them, suddenly, without warning, a form of reaction, perhaps, from the calculated unreality of the world I had just left, I knew that I was going to fall in love with all of them.

With Laura Bailey there was no hesitation, it was love at first sight, a phenomenon which occurs more frequently in

21

married men as they grow older and more depressed by confinement. She was, I suppose, about thirty. Barely so. If she was not beautiful someone else would have had to tell me that, for in my eyes she seemed quite perfect. She had that wonderful confidence of young American women, a confidence which Europeans sometimes find necessary to be critical about, and which even American men sometimes find dismaying, but there it is, and there they are, and they are ours. She was long-limbed and fully-fleshed. One thought of how Michelangelo would have loved her for a model, for one of those voluptuously reclining figures, perhaps, with which he decorated the tombs of the Medici, although it was difficult to think of Laura Bailey being still long enough for that, even for Michelangelo. She had dark hair which hung free to her shoulders, and she moved with grace, and her wonderful confidence was, as one could see, the product of intelligence and compassion, and of her utter joy in her role in life.

We exchanged introductions, greetings, banalities, and in those few moments little Billy succeeded in tying himself up in a pear tree. Little Billy, who had responded to the question about his age by holding up four fingers, had come dressed in a fringed jacket, blue denims, cowboy boots, a cowboy hat, and a lariat. Through some effort, which I wished I had observed, he was now suspended by one foot and one arm from our small pear tree in a tangle of rope, head downward above the ground, as helpless as Antaeus, and from the confusion of fringe, hat, and rope there now issued a small voice which said, "Mother."

It was not a cry for help. It was not a cry of alarm. It was a simple statement, the necessary statement of a man who finds that he has made a fool of himself in public and wishes to be extricated from the situation with as little attention as

22

possible. I recognized Billy then for what he was: Everyman, hoist with his own petard; Charlie Chaplin poised above the banana peel; Buster Keaton with pie on his face.

"Oh, Billy," Laura said with mild exasperation, as she went to free him. Once released, Billy skipped away, humming a little tune, as if to deny that the whole episode had taken place.

Suzy, Laura's daughter, had clung to her mother's skirt throughout everything. One thumb was in her mouth. Her other hand was tangled sleepily in her hair. Suzy was dark, with lustrous eyes, and she was two, but she did not speak. Not yet.

"Suzy will speak when she makes up her mind that she wants to," Laura said, caressing Suzy's hair. There was in her fond tone not only that wonderful confidence but also the suggestion of an unshakable belief in her ability to cope with anything. I believed that she could. We had yet to meet Tim Bailey, her husband, but already I had a feeling that I knew what he was like. How right I was about that, and how very wrong, all lay ahead, but one had the feeling that whoever he was or whatever he was, his marriage to Laura was inevitable. I don't pretend to know very much about the marriages of young people in our country as we find ourselves well advanced, however falteringly, into the second half of the twentieth century, but it does seem to me that if marriage is a state of mutual dependence, then the nature of that dependence has shifted in my time. Much more in terms of practical effort seems to be required of women. Much more uncertainty seems to be the lot of men.

And I could see, as we chatted, how Kate had also been captured by Laura. With women, just as with men, there are those who sometimes recognize each other instantly as friends.

Friendship between members of the same sex is rather difficult to describe. Any writer will tell you that. It is somehow easier to write of love than of friendship, and, I suppose, for a variety of reasons. Love is a physical attraction, it is unpredictable, and it may not last. Lovers very seldom stop to examine the world around them, or to discover, often until it is too late, what tastes or likes they share in common. Friendship is a much more critical relationship. Very often it is much more stable and enduring than love, and it can be in the end more satisfying. It has been my superficial observation, possibly an incorrect one, that friendship between women begins with an instinctive knowledge of what the other dislikes, and it is this sharing of dislikes, or this rejection of the taste and the behavior of others, that forms the basic foundation of their friendship.

Shortly after our marriage I had once gone with Kate to a reunion of her class at the college she had attended. Kate had been undecided about going to the reunion. She didn't really want to go, she said. She hated reunions and things like that. But it had been a special reunion of some kind, and she had been persuaded to go, sappy as it probably would be, but after we got there she had a wonderful time, principally because two or three of her old classmates who didn't like reunions either and wouldn't have been caught dead at one were there also, and what wicked fun they had, examining at close range, from the comfort of their own society, all those other classmates of theirs who did enjoy reunions and even went to them!

I learned then that one of the most damning things that could be said of those hopeless women was that they had been "girly" girls. I never did find out exactly what that meant because it couldn't be explained. Either you knew what a girly girl was or you didn't, and if you didn't, why bother to explain, because that probably meant that you were also hopeless. Girly girls did "sissy" things. That was the best I could do. To this day the whole thing remains for me in the category of those feminine mysteries which are guarded by the priestesses in the sanctuary of Diana.

But let us say that Laura Bailey was not a girly girl. Even if she and Kate were separated in years by almost a generation it did not matter. They were women, and they were ladies, but they were not sissies and they met on common ground.

"Billy wants me to ask you if he may run on your lawn," Laura said. "It's bigger than ours, and there won't be any sandbox or playpen in the way. He says he will run errands for you if you will let him run on the lawn."

"Oh, my dear," Kate said, "of course Billy may run on our lawn! He may run on our lawn as much as he likes. But he must not feel that he has to do anything in return."

"Oh, he wants to," Laura said, taking Suzy's hand and turning back to their house. "He would like to."

We parted. We told Laura how delighted we were to have them as neighbors. We went back to our house. I reviewed for Kate as we walked across the lawn how the meeting had gone with Alton Tweed's agent. I told her I couldn't see myself doing that at all. "But I'm still not off the hook," I said. "Bert is going to set up an appointment with the next producer on his list."

"Maybe you will like the next one better," Kate said. "Maybe you might enjoy the whole thing once you were in it. It may not be as difficult and unpleasant as it sounds." That was what she said, but her voice had that rather absent quality that the voices of writers' wives acquire after a while, subject as those women are to a lifetime of creative indecision.

"Oh, I'll meet anyone with an open mind," I said, looking up at the old house and thinking that the foremost advantage of these proposals was that they helped postpone any important decision about future plans.

Kate looked up at the old house too. She sighed.

CHAPTER TWO

WE had come to the old house just after World War II. Everyone was just home from the war, everyone was young, everyone was a veteran, and life was beginning again, with all of the privileges and excitement that estate provided. It had been our world. Nothing could go wrong. Every decision we made was as chiseled with our young self-confidence as if it had been cut into marble. We bought the old house without a moment's hesitation after one look at it. We were ready to take up our life again where the war had interrupted it. We never looked back at anything. We had energy to spare for every purpose, and almost everything in life amused us. Everything was still ahead.

The house was a full Victorian house. Great-grandfather Hopkins, of the family from whom we had bought the old house, had added the other half just after the Civil War, the parlor with its plaster cornices and ceiling medallions, the library beyond, the three bedrooms above. But over the years the family had diminished and scattered. The house had been neglected. After we had lived in it for a while someone in the village told us that it was the one house no one had ever

27

wanted to buy. But that would not have dismayed us then. We loved it as it was. It had not been painted for a long time and the last coat of green paint had faded to a sort of pea-soup shade. The paint could be rubbed away like chalk. The house had been adorned at one time with elaborate scrollwork around the eaves and outlining the Florentine arches of the pillars which held up the porch roof, the sort of architectural detail which had given to the houses of the area the name of Hudson River Bracketed. On summer afternoons awnings had once shaded the shuttered windows, as we saw in a large photograph, sepia, framed, pocked with fox-marks, which we found in the dusty attic. In this photograph a flag flew from a flagstaff which extended out over a bay window, and on a wide lawn planted with beds of calla lilies, ladies in shirt-waist dresses and long skirts played croquet with gentlemen who wore tight-waisted jackets and bowler hats and moustaches.

All of this had vanished, along with the scrollwork, by the time we bought the house. Nothing remained but its fine old bones, covered with fading, chalky paint. It seemed to sit on the level of the road which ran along in front of it, but from the meadow in back you saw that actually it sat upon a slight rise in its spare glory, the elimination of detail seeming to be the sort of thing that a Chinese artist might have done to reveal the elementary beauty. From the meadow one could watch the setting sun strike gold from its windows.

We came to the house in winter, and even though it snowed all that day we thought of that as hardly anything more than an added diversion, although I think the men on the moving van were not so entertained. The snow stopped sometime during the night and on our first morning we wakened to a rose-colored reflection on the ceiling above us, in our uncurtained room, from the sun on the snow outside. We thought we had gone to heaven. And there all about us was the old house, stripped to its essentials, waiting for us to put our mark on it.

Or to give it our smell, as Kate would have said. Kate was a woman who loved the senses. When you had been away and had come back, she would rush to your arms and say, "Let me smell you." And she didn't mean the scent of your after-shave lotion. Nothing displeased her more than a scent meant to disguise an honest smell, or one posing as one that it wasn't. The house had an old smell, but it was not an unpleasant smell. On damp days the chimneys in the parlor and the dining room sent out smells of past fires in the fireplaces, and the sandalwood scent of old wood greeted you as you opened the front door.

There was even a psychic-phenomenon smell. Naturally the house had its ghost, as any self-respecting house of the period did. Our chief ghost-in-residence opened our bedroom door on nights of the full moon, slowly, with that creaking sound used in motion pictures of suspense. We would lie in bed and watch it, with differing reactions. My reaction was a sort of proprietary delight. There had been a ghost in the house where I had spent my childhood, who had walked the verandah at night, and I felt that now I really had it made, to be the owner of a house with a ghost of its own. But Kate, whose delight in the senses stopped short of the supernatural, had a more practical point of view, and she took some satisfaction in pointing out to me, after the new furnace had been installed and the old beams had been thoroughly dried out, that our ghost seemed to have gone to other haunts. But she had never been able to explain away the ghost-scent of fresh bread and freshly brewed coffee which wakened guests who slept in the back bedroom, even before anyone was downstairs in the kitchen. It did not vanish with the installation of the

29

new furnace, and I think that practical Kate finally came to delight in it herself. As she said, it was at the hour when the lady of the house would have had to be up to prepare breakfast for the men, in the days when the old house had been supported by the produce grown in its fields, and surely only a happy ghost would return for such duties.

We had been the happy ghosts in our own turn, moving about in the old house, making it our own, creating our own past there, giving it our smell. What incredible energy Kate had poured into that! She had planned the gardens and planted them. She had planted miles of pachysandra, and nourished it and cared for it. She had painted steps and doors and walls, and among my most vivid memories I had the picture of her putting the dining room walls together with her hands, when she had discovered that what was under the old wallpaper was not plaster, but daub and wattle, the lime and animal hair of an earlier day, which she had repaired and smoothed and spackled with all the loving concentration of a child making mud pies.

And what of the parties she had given? And the guest children sleeping in upstairs rooms? The fragrance of bacon and coffee, substantial and unghostly, on a summer morning, with the scent of roses or lilies coming in through the open windows? Or wintry mornings, in our first days in the old house, when Kate had been reluctant to give up the old wood range in the corner of the kitchen, even after the gas stove had been installed, because, as she said, it was always so comforting to have something simmering on the back of the stove. It had still sat there, untended, through the summer, but when the first cool days of fall came it was stoked again, and Cam, coming home from school, had put his books down there, not knowing it was lighted, and had scorched his spelling book, thus making more of an impression on the book, I think, than the book had made on him.

When I thought of Kate in the rooms there, endlessly busy, endlessly occupied with the details of housekeeping, endlessly cleaning, setting the table, arranging flowers, or finally sitting on the sofa after dinner with her shoes off and her toes curled under her, sipping coffee, while Cam brought back to us his tales of first ventures into the great world, I could not think of her in any other place. My heart stopped with her there. That was the way it had been. That was our life.

"Oh, I love the old house," Kate said, when we were left alone in it. "I've always *loved* it. But I just don't like it any more. I want to get away."

We could not speak further. We could not look at each other. We turned away for a moment, until we had picked up our inward thoughts again, and placed them safely away behind our eyes.

Some people we knew rented their houses when they were left alone, and went off to live in Florida, or Arizona, or to an apartment in New York. They sometimes even rented their houses furnished, which seemed fairly easy to do in this day when so many people seemed temporarily on the move. There were certain advantages to this, with the income from the rent, and the house maintained in your absence, but it was an evasion, really, not any final solution to the problem, with the added care of being an absentee landlord, which didn't exactly appeal to us. And the real headache about renting, as Kate said, was that you had to clear out all of the closets and the bureau drawers.

The closets and the bureau drawers were a kind of symbol. Our life was in them, and that was what was troubling us. What was our life? We were alone in a house that was too big for us, but where did we want to go? We were still in the

31

vigorous middle years of our life, and what did we want from life?

The latter question was one, perhaps, which would only re-solve itself in the doing, but the primary question of the house required a decision, a decision which had faced us ever since Nancy and Cam had gone away from us with little John. I thought often of our final evening together, and I invoked the memory of that to see if any clue to the solution was pres-ent at that time of departure.

It was early evening and Nancy and Cam had come to our house for dinner. John had been fed and he was taken up-stairs, nodding with sleep, to be put down on a bed, and hedged about with pillows. Nancy and Cam had decided that after dinner they would get in the car and start off on their trip. It was not a step which I would have recommended, but one of the many things I had learned as the father of a mar-ried man was at least not to recommend. The movers had come and emptied the Harbinger gate house where Nancy and Cam had lived since the birth of little John. We had thought to share them as neighbors for several years, while Cam worked toward the degree he had failed to get the first time around, before he had gone into the service. But he had been recruited away in less than a year by the enterprising representative of one of those monolithic concerns which we had learned to refer to just as the company. In another age the allegiance of a young man of family might have been to the land, to the family who lived on that land and whom he would one day supplant, but now the allegiance of every young man of parts was to the company. It was a new form of paternalism. The company would take care of everything. The company did not even find it necessary to wait until Cam had finished slogging toward that delayed degree. What college courses he had completed before going into the service, together with the technical experience he had gained there, was enough for them. They would now mold him into what they wanted of him, with special training as necessary, and the offer they had made him was impossible to resist for a young man who had impulsively acquired a wife and a son.

A year of marriage had changed Cam and Nancy, and I don't mean in any superficial way of outlook or maturity, although it had done its share of that. They seemed somehow different in the flesh, as if the physical act of loving had brought about some cellular change. Perhaps it does, perhaps it does. Cam had always been a healthy boy, and he was a healthy young man, but what used to be described as the rude look of health, the high color in the cheeks, the rough textured hands, the mouth, wind-chapped and raw in color— this had all somehow subsided and melded and a new color had risen from within, a sort of olive tone to the flesh, consistent and mellow, as if he had cast a skin to reveal a new skin grown beneath. He was pleasant to look at. He had a finished look, and a quiet sense of authority about him, as if whatever it was he had to prove to himself had been proven, and when he looked at Nancy and she returned that look, one sometimes had a glimpse of another continent upon which it would never be our privilege to set foot.

A change somehow similar had taken place in Nancy. While she had never quite possessed that measure of self-confidence which had been given, for example, to Laura Bailey, hers was a different nature, with different needs. She was more dependent. She needed Cam, and it was her need of Cam that Cam needed.

I had once asked Nancy, just in idle conversation, what had made her accept Cam. For me it was a rhetorical question, I suppose. I was prejudiced. I couldn't imagine any girl anywhere who wouldn't want Cam. I suppose for that reason her answer surprised me. "Oh, I had just about given up finding any man I wanted to marry," Nancy said. "They all seemed just like little boys, and I couldn't imagine spending the rest of my life taking over where their mothers had left off. But when I met Cam the first thing I saw about him was his overt security."

Overt security? The language of the young today is often baffling, especially if they have taken any courses in college in education or psychology, or any of the other essentially unnecessary disciplines. Overt, for me, was one of those words I kept tucked away in a drawer, along with tie tacks and watch fobs and other things I never got around to using. But I nodded gravely at Nancy's revelation, and as soon as I could get away I went to a dictionary. "Overt," it said. "Open to view, public, apparent, manifest." What a lucky man Cam was, I thought, to have a wife who saw security every time she looked at him, right out there in public, open to view! It even changed my way of looking at Cam. Sometimes parents can't see the forest because of the trees, and all those little saplings of untidiness, procrastination, natural rebellion and stubbornness had apparently obscured for me what a true giant of a man Cam was.

Nancy too had changed in the flesh. From their separate flesh they had produced another flesh, and this seemed to have fortified them, to have invested them with greater substance. Particularly Nancy. Her girlish awkwardness had vanished. She now seemed as rounded and as smooth and as indestructible as a figure of a woman by Maillol. There was a lustrous, burnished look about her, just as the leaves of the young cherry tree grow more brilliant after it first bears fruit.

They were high-keyed and happy as they sat with us at dinner. It had been an exhausting day, an emotional day for all of us. We had stayed away from the little house with its dia-mond-paned windows, and its little bedrooms under the eaves where we had so happily seen them established the year be-fore. We didn't want to go there. We wouldn't have been needed if we had gone. The company had taken care of every-thing.

"But I did want to wrap my precious things myself," Nancy said. And then she began to laugh, thinking of a funny story the wife of one of Cam's new business associates had told her, at a party they had been invited to, to look at, and to be looked at. It seemed that before the movers had come for this particular company wife she had made sandwiches for herself and her husband, of bacon, lettuce and tomato. She had put the discarded lettuce leaves and the trimmings of the tomato into the little triangular plastic garbage container which sat in the corner of her sink.

"And when they moved into their new house, seven hun-dred and fifty miles away," Nancy said, over her laughter, "there in the corner of her new sink was the old garbage con-tainer, with the withered lettuce leaves and tomato trimmings still inside!"

We laughed at that. It was good to have something to laugh at in an evening so filled with emotion. They ate their dinner. They were eager to be off. Now that their house was empty they wanted to be on their way. They thanked Kate for her offer, indeed her plea, that they stay the night and begin their journey in the morning. No, with the baby it was just too much. If they were to unpack his crib and bring out all of his equipment they might as well do it in a motel where they would be already on their way.

We waved them off from the porch. We resisted emotional goodbyes. We would be coming out to see them. They would be coming back to see us. Life is that way. It is a series of departures, which, even if they are possibly a part of natural growth, are like small deaths, not easy to endure.

Kate went on up to bed. I fixed myself a drink, a nightcap, and settled down in the living room, the old parlor. I wasn't quite ready for sleep. Often I liked to sit up like this with the house, as if it were an old friend. We had grown older together. The house was twenty years older now than it was when we had moved into it, and so was I. Of course, the house had been much older to begin with. But it had served us well. It had given us roots. We had said we were looking for them when we had moved from the city. And we did have roots, all of us. Cam could go anywhere with confidence, as he had gone now, because he left from a point of departure. We were that point of departure. The neighbors, the village, the friends all about who had provided him with his life experience, deeply rooted in memory, they were his point of departure.

Surely this could not be lightly dismissed. If we are to maintain a culture in our society surely we must have a gentle reverence for the pattern of living, unless we are all to turn into airborne plants, as transitory and as irresponsible as Spanish moss. We felt a responsibility to this. Although we never, I think, expressed it in so many words, we did feel a sense of responsibility to the pattern of life in which Cam's roots had been nurtured and in which he had grown. As far away as he might go from us we did not want him ever to feel that the past was cut away from him and that he was condemned to wander the country forever with his withered lettuce leaves and his tomato trimmings, with no place to return to, no place to bring his family home.

Yet just what were the boundaries of our responsibility to the milieu in which we had brought up a son? The old house was too big for us. It was expensive to maintain, and it was

36

difficult to maintain. The disintegration of an old house is a gradual process, presumably like mortal aging itself. As with the scrollwork around the eaves and the Florentine arches of the early house, bits and pieces fall off here and there like frosting from a cake. Window sills and door sills decay in the sun. The mortar between the bricks of the chimneys erodes in the wind and the rain. Screens warp, paint chips. An old house needs an attendant, and you had better learn to be that attendant yourself. Letting your fingers take a walk through the yellow pages isn't going to help very much, for you will soon find that the best of the young men have also gone off to work for the company, and those who are left behind to do the odd jobs are very odd indeed.

I got up from my chair to make my customary nightly rounds, to check the doors and turn off the lights, to look out of the windows at the darkness and the stars, before I went on up to bed. I felt angry that a decision was required of me, as now it seemed to be, when I felt emotionally incapable of making it. I loved the old house. I never wanted to leave. And yet perhaps it was impractical or even irresponsible of us to stay there. Who is in charge here? I wanted to say.

We were. It was a decision we would have to make for ourselves.

CHAPTER THREE

AFTER my experience with the assistant of Alton Tweed, I was unprepared for the charm of Maxim Benton, producer number two, although it was possible that nothing could have prepared anyone for the charm of Mr. Benton. He was young, fair, beautiful and damned, and although I had never met him I had heard it said that he had been rejected by every reputable psychiatrist in New York, on the ground that only his neuroses held him together, in much the same manner that certain old houses are said to remain upright only because the termites clasp hands.

Through Mr. Benton I became introduced to the genus *theatrical producer*. They are not mere mortals, theatrical producers, even as you and I. They are driven by private furies, and their glands are different. They have little dynamos inside that tick away twenty-four hours a day, and, as with nature herself, the only thing they abhor is a vacuum. They absolutely must be involved in at least six projects at one time, and preferably more. Other people of mortal stature who are caught up in these projects sometimes die, or have heart attacks, or are taken off to private sanatoriums and never heard of again, but the theatrical producer, who might have to think twice for the answer if you were suddenly to ask him to name the President of the United States, would be happily in Tel Aviv arranging a revival of one of his productions, or in London signing a new star, or possibly getting a road company together for his latest hit, meanwhile involved in at least three law suits, which he had either brought, or which had been brought against him. This was Maxim Benton, the newest meteor in the Broadway firmament; shining teeth, blue eyes, sun-bleached hair, a perpetual tan, in flannels and shoes from London.

Furthermore, in a way that endeared him most to me, he said that he loved my novel, hereinafter referred to as the property, which had begun again to glow softly in the dark. It had kept him up all night reading it. He absolutely could not put it down. He was filled with brilliant ideas of how it should be done in the theater.

This he told to us, Bert and me, in his apartment with terrace in Manhattan, high over the East River. Mr. Benton, known as Max, had furnished his apartment with the refuse of vanished cultures, mostly broken bits of Gothic church sculpture. Fingers and hands, and fragments of saintly pelvis in polychromed wood were everywhere, and in the middle of all of this sat Max on a hassock, like a pixie on a toadstool, to talk about the property.

"God, I need a drink," he said, after the mutual admiration society had begun its meeting. He leapt from the hassock as if jerked by invisible wires, and went to the corner of the room where the bar was concealed behind Gothic linen-fold paneling which had seen much better days. There he poured for each of us a tumbler of whiskey, and handed them around the room like glasses of tea.

"And now," he said, resuming his attitude of perpetual

39

torment on the hassock, "I will tell you what I see in the property."

He did. The ensuing monologue was the most brilliant performance I had ever witnessed. Not only had Max Benton read the novel, he knew every line of it, inside out, and backward and forward. He knew not only what was in each line, but what was behind each line, and above it and below it. He knew the characters of the novel better than I did who had written it, and he knew their motives, which had never been really clear to me. I had a suspicion as he talked that he probably even knew me better than I knew myself. He saw the whole play finished, complete, done, produced, performed and running forever. All that I had to do was to write it and collect a million dollars. Would I do that?

To my infinite astonishment, I would.

And now I was back in my study in the old house, with all uncertainty vanquished. We were once more happily ensconced in the universe, with our new neighbors next door, whom we felt we had known forever. I was writing a play. The dreamlike days fled by. I even began to think of myself with a new dimension. I was now a novelist and a playwright. I was also sometimes a man in trouble, in a way I could only compare to that of being faced with a plateful of spaghetti for the first time. Strands of the work would sometimes slip away just when I thought I had them firmly wound around the fork. To write dialogue for people moving about a room was not at all the same as writing dialogue and a description of that room to be read from a page. Ends dangled. On bad days suddenly the whole mass might grow cold and congeal in front of me.

In such a circumstance, even when I was writing a novel and bogged down, it was my custom to go outside and garden, or work around the house. Now I had the good fortune to be joined in these forays by Billy Bailey, who took my appearance outside as a signal to join me. Billy would dance about, interfering, which was referred to as helping, and on one such afternoon he waited for me to tell me that he had found a dead bird. It was a blue jay, unmarked, but unmistakably dead, and I went to the barn for a spade. We buried him near the yew hedge, where Billy had found him, and when we had covered him with earth we hid his grave with leaves. I said, "Good night, sweet prince, and flights of angels sing thee to thy rest," and Billy said, "Do you pray for a bird?" I said, "Of course. The birds are God's creatures, even as you and I," and suddenly I felt ancient, not in years, but in behavior, as if I were handing down, if not wisdom or belief, at least some custom or ritual bred into my bones.

I did not get to know Billy well until later, but even from the first we could look at each other directly in a way I had found difficult to do sometimes with my own son when he was a boy. The relationship of father to son is a very complex one, and often a great deal of time is taken up by evasion, by hiding from each other, in a way which seems necessary for survival. The secrets of one's own identity are never more vulnerable, never nearer to exposure, never more threatened than they are in those confrontations between father and son. But Billy and I could survive without hiding secrets from each other. We could look at each other. There was so much we had to learn from each other, and I suppose that also I saw in Billy a surrogate for my own grandson, so far away, still an infant, who had not yet brought me a dead bird to bury.

Just as we had finished our ritual at the yew hedge, Tim Bailey whirled into the driveway next door, in the little Volkswagen he drove to his office, that tiny car so unaccountably preferred by our larger young men. We had not talked as yet, but he gave us a wave when he had unfolded himself from the car, and he slammed the door, and made his way into the house.

"I have to go now," Billy said. "I have to go home because my father hasn't seen me yet today."

Not, "I haven't seen my father yet today," I mused, standing there, but, "My father hasn't seen me yet today." Billy rushed away across the lawn, toward the complexity of that relationship which would never be resolved in the lifetime of either one of them.

And then there were other distractions, other interruptions in my fledgling days as a playwright. The Dramatists Guild, which had never existed before for me anywhere except in the telephone book, now decided to be firm. The Dramatists Guild, it seems, did not go all starry-eyed with wonder, as I did, at the mention of Maxim Benton's name. All was not entirely well with the contract he had submitted. There was something wrong with paragraph two of clause B. Along the way lurked further pitfalls which would require much study and discussion, and in my best interests the check Mr. Benton had made out to me to hold an option on the property would not be cleared until all of these ambiguities were resolved. Since writers are assumed to be above financial considerations, the work went on anyway. Certainly I was of no help with the contract, since I had never seen a contract for a play before. In its orange paper binding the contract weighed approximately eight ounces, and when it had been sent to me for observation I had sent it back to Bert Thompson by return mail, with the explanation that I could either read the contract or try to write the play, but that I could not do both, at least not in the same year.

Bert's answer to this was to telephone me at helpful intervals, to keep me, as he said, posted, a form of torment roughly like that of Chinese water torture, during which he might talk to me for as long as twenty-five minutes without stopping, about TV package deals, road company rights, foreign productions, Hollywood options, information which I tried, unsuccessfully, to understand, since the characters of my play, enwound in their strands of spaghetti, had the lamentable habit of going on talking, too.

There were days, also, when Max Benton himself would materialize, without any advance notice, and certainly without any reference to such vulgar subjects as money or contracts. He had merely come, as he said, to see how things were going.

He drove a small open sports car, shaped rather like the discarded shell of a cicada, and on these excursions he would be accompanied by some luminary of the theater, an actor or actress with a face so familiar or so famous that it had long since ceased to be mortal; trailing wisps of glory or notoriety, they would invade our quiet retreat, and while Kate disappeared, to attempt a metamorphosis from her gardening or kitchen appearance, I would emerge, blinking, from my solitary confinement, to get out ice and liquor and other components of the good life.

Max did not really want to know how the playscript was going, other than to be reassured that I was working on it. He did not want to discuss it, he said, until it was finished. Writing a play was a problem in architecture. A delicate problem. It was like building a summer house, or a gazebo. Especially when the play in question was a comedy. It must soar. It must seem not to touch the earth. If you took out a beam, or a strut, or whatever it was that architects used in building, to examine it, the whole thing might collapse, just like a soufflé. An architectural soufflé.

43

No, we would just visit. We would just talk. We would gossip. On the lawn or in the living room, while vodka and tonic flowed, famous personages, known to us only through the gossip columns of the press, were drawn and quartered in absentia, and their bloody corpses strewn about. It was all very amusing. We would laugh. We would laugh until our teeth ached and our temples throbbed, and then it was up, up and away, and they were off, in the little discarded cicada shell, trailing scents of exhaust fumes and essence of Yves St. Laurent.

"Keep going!" Max would call. "Onward and upward! I'll be in touch!"

I'll be in touch. Don't call me, I'll call you. In the theater it is the death knell of hope. Or, as John Greenleaf Whittier put it, "For of all sad words of tongue or pen/ The saddest are these: 'It might have been!' "

It was just when I had the playscript finished that Max Benton disappeared. He simply vanished into the woodwork. His office professed not to know where he was. His unlisted number at his apartment had been changed.

"They do this every once in a while," Bert said. "They're all alike. There isn't anything you can do about it. We'll just have to sit it out."

It wasn't easy to sit it out. I had actually gone and done it, against my better judgment. I had actually written a play. Now I wanted to go on to the next step. I wanted to see it in rehearsal. I wanted actors hired. I wanted Max Benton to look at the script. Hadn't he said he loved the property? Hadn't he sat up all night to read the novel? Weren't we friends? Didn't we sit and exchange gossip about the great? The ticking sound in the background was the passing of the days under which Max Benton held an option on the property.

44

And then one day, inevitably, the ticking stopped, like an egg-timer run its course, and all at once the beautiful half-pound contract with its initialed clauses and its orange paper binding was as worthless as the paper on which it was printed. The Dramatists Guild hadn't even released the check.

The telephone rang as I sat there staring at the calendar. It was Bert. "I suppose he just got interested in something else," he said. "That happens all the time. But Serge Lichtenstein wants to see you. He's just been waiting for the option to lapse. He says he trained Max Benton for the theater, you know, and Max has never given him any credit for this, so he's dying to show him up. After all, you've got the script finished. What have you got to lose?"

Numbly I made a date. Numbly I replaced the telephone. And at this moment Kate called to me. Kate never interrupted me at my work. It was the first rule of the house, which she scrupulously observed without even any mention of it. But she had heard the telephone ring. She had known that I had answered it. And now she was at my study door with the sound of excitement in her voice. I asked her to come in.

She had the morning newspaper in her hand. "Look," she said. "Did you see this?"

I hadn't looked at the paper that morning, being too preoccupied to care. Now I took it from Kate to read the item she indicated. The heading read, "Cliffside Man Jailed." The Cliffside man, it turned out, was our new neighbor, Tim Bailey, and he had been arrested for lying down to block the doorway of a chemical plant where napalm gas was said to be manufactured. He had been with a group of anti-war demonstrators, and the others had moved on when ordered to do so, but Mr. Timothy Bailey had remained there, prone, until he was lifted by police into a police van, and taken off to be booked.

"What do you think of that?" Kate said.

"I don't think anything about it," I said. "All I can think about is that Max Benton has let the option lapse on the play, and now I have to go to see somebody named Serge Lichtenstein."

CHAPTER FOUR

SERGE LICHTENSTEIN, producer, director, entrepreneur, a survival of the days of silent films who wished to be called by his first name, which was not pronounced serge, as in blue serge suit, but sir-gay, was indeed, as he liked to be told, a legend in his time. The devil with whom he had made his pact was either unusually patient, or else the stakes they played for were extremely high, since it was obvious that we were going to have Mr. Lichtenstein with us for some time, whether we wanted it that way or not.

It was impossible to determine his antecedents. He had a sort of do-it-yourself accent which was not quite placeable, and sounded, as I later heard someone say, like the sort of accent a man might make up to disguise himself. It seemed, at various times, Russian, German, or even French, and at times like none of these, which sometimes led me to believe that he had either come from a country he had made up for himself, or that he hadn't been born at all, but had sprung full-blown from the brow of the late Max Reinhardt.

There were those who said he made a career out of failure, trumpeting his own name so loudly that he drowned out the

47

cries of the critics, but I didn't know that at the time. The man I met, an imposing man with a strong and worldly face, seemed capable of anything. His aroma was, if not of success, at least of self-confidence, mingled with the scent of vintage wines, sauce Béarnaise, cologne, and expensive women. His handshake was firm, his smile beatific. "We will make a success together," he said. I cannot approximate his accent, and I will not try, except to say that there were no *w*'s in his alphabet, and the whole thing came out with a slightly glottal sound, but that only seemed to make the statement more emphatic. We shook hands and agreed.

The script, of course, would have to be done over again from the beginning. The whimsy I had created for Max Benton was the sort of thing from which one recoiled. Naturally, it all should be done realistically, since it was a play about real people. Of course it would still be a comedy, but it would be a straight comedy. And there would be ample time for rewriting, for, as with any other producer, Serge was involved in six other projects. He had to make a quick flight to London to confer with his backers about a film he was shooting in France. A director was coming from Hollywood to be coached in a revival of a play that would open in Berlin. There would be time.

And this time Kate and I decided to spend in New York. If there was any disappearing to be done, we wanted to be on hand to witness the performance. Also, *mirabile dictu,* the Dramatists Guild, which had punished me for working for Max Benton by withholding his check, instantly approved a contract with Serge Lichtenstein, and I found myself holding his option money in my hand.

Unfortunately, one of the many bits of information which had failed to make its way to us in our twenty years of absence from life in New York was that suddenly everyone else had a great deal of money. In those years we had, of course, gone into town for dinner or the theater on occasion, perhaps not as often as we might have liked, and I suppose the gradually rising costs of these excursions should have been some warning to us, but the joys and disasters of parenthood had blinded us to other concerns. To live in New York City now seemed to imply an income beyond the dreams of avarice, although it was apparent, even at a cursory glance, that there was plenty of avarice still around.

It was possible to sublet a furnished private apartment in New York, but just as we did not cherish the idea of emptying our own closets and bureau drawers, so we did not really like the prospect of sharing others temporarily cleared for us. It seemed unnecessary for a period of a few months to fit ourselves into another's way of life. An apartment hotel seemed the answer, although we really did not know who lived in them. I suppose we thought of them as existing for people like ourselves, who wanted to spend a season in town.

A tour of the more respectable apartment hotels quickly disabused us of this notion. Although once they may have done so, mere people no longer lived in these rooms and suites. They were now opulent caravansaries for the fleeting visits of executive vice-presidents in charge of sales, for the entertainment of other executive vice-presidents in charge of sales, and the prices quoted undoubtedly included champagne and call girls. It came as quite a shock to discover that a whole group of beings had come into existence who never soiled their fingers with the vulgar currency we used, but who eased their entire way through life with a collection of plastic-coated credit cards, all redeemable by the company. Since we had only mere money to get by on, we ended up at the Hotel Eden.

The Hotel Eden wasn't the most expensive residential

49

hotel, and it wasn't the least. It was possible that it had known more respectable days, but who hadn't? A sensible management might have had the grace to change its name, but a sensible management would, I think, have walked off quickly in the opposite direction after one look at it.

In its favor, it was constructed in the days of vintage building in New York, when walls were sound, and ceilings were high, and closets and bathrooms were large. It was on the west side of Central Park, which roughly corresponded to being on the wrong side of the railroad tracks, but the trees and the shrubbery in the park on the west side looked the same as did the trees and shrubbery on the east side. It was impossible to walk in the park at night, or at least not recommended, but you couldn't walk in the park on the east side either, for the same reason, at twice the price.

Actually, it wasn't bad. Kate was ready for it, and she loved it. And from the Hotel Eden we would have a vantage point to study New York City again. Perhaps that was where we belonged after all, now that our cycle of parenthood was apparently completed. While I worked at my play, we could see what it was like to live there.

"It's sort of like Paris," Kate said, standing at our bedroom window, which looked down upon the chimney pots of a row of brownstone houses on the street beyond. It was possibly even more like Paris from the windows of our living room, which looked across the street to the park and its trees, the tracery of their branches revealed against the early winter sky. Even the sounds of the sirens of the police cars and the fire engines, which filled the streets by day and by night, seemed rather exciting, at least at first; a city noise, just as the clanking of the garbage cans at dawn was a city noise, created by men who had obviously been trained to get all the noise that it was possible to get out of a garbage-can lid. When I was a boy we had sometimes played at knights in armor, using the lids of garbage cans as shields, and while I never got up to check, it was my impression that the garbage men of New York were chosen from that retarded group who had never been able to get past this step of boyish development, and jousted each morning in the streets in garbage-can armor, in emulation of King Arthur and his court.

The apartment itself consisted of a small foyer, a living room, a bedroom, and a bath. Beyond the foyer as one came into the apartment was a door leading into something called a serving pantry, a name which was actually a euphemism for kitchen, since meals could be prepared there, but in a cheating sort of way, since it really wasn't a kitchen. What it really was I don't think anyone knew. The serving pantry was about the size of a closet. You could close the door from inside once you were inside, but this was not advised, since it meant instant claustrophobia. The door to the serving pantry had been cut in half, in the manner of those doors called Dutch doors, and the thing to do was to go inside the serving pantry, close the lower half of the door, and raise the shelf attached to the inside of the door to create a little working space. Inside the serving pantry was a small sink, with shelves above. Next to the sink was a counter on which there was a two-burner electric hot-plate. A refrigerator sat in the corner, and the whole tasteful decor was completed by the fuse box attached to the wall, actually the most important piece of equipment, since if the refrigerator just happened to turn itself on to refrigerate while the electric hot-plate was on, or while the toaster was on, everything went off together. If it had been possible to buy fuses by the gross I would have bought them that way. As it was, I kept them stacked in every corner, for one of the few stratagems Kate was unable to master while we were at the Hotel Eden was to brew a pot of coffee, toast a slice of bread, and fry bacon, all at the same time, without blowing the whole thing. Yes, it was just like Paris.

But it was a comfortable place. There was wall-to-wall carpeting, an alien luxury to us, since wall-to-wall carpeting was considered rather vulgar in the country. We went about a great deal in our stocking feet, a pleasure denied to us at home since old floors have a way of splintering. The apartment was furnished in what might be described as international hotel modern, chairs and sofa vaguely Scandinavian in design, but easy to sit in and read or relax. The beds in the bedroom were a pleasure, there were many lamps and bureaus and a dressing table for Kate, and the bathroom was, as she said, just like the bathrooms at Atlantic City, big, old-fashioned, with lots of white tile and lots of hot water and a big tub to soak in. It was early January when we arrived at the Hotel Eden, after a rather lonesome Christmas at home, and what we did for the first few days was comfort ourselves with the knowledge that everything for our comfort was being done by someone else, and that even when it snowed the snow did not fall for us to clear away, but for the New York City sanitation department, or for the staff of the hotel.

The staff of the hotel also included Alma, who came to clean each morning, and to make the beds, a circumstance which did a great deal to contribute to Kate's comfort. It was Alma, however, who finally drove me forth from paradise. Alma was a New York Negro, born and bred, a species unto itself. Outside, and all across the country, disturbances were raging in the name of civil rights, but Alma didn't want to speak about that. You could be sure that Alma would stand up to be counted when it came to a question of her civil rights because she was, after all, a New Yorker, and they don't come any more enterprising than that, but Alma had Ralph her husband, and little Betsy her daughter, and that was bliss for her, and that was what she wanted to talk about. She began when she came into the apartment in the morning, burdened with linens and soap and mops and brushes. It was like a daily television serial. We opened with quotations from the wit and wisdom of little Betsy, who, at age three, might have kept Art Linkletter supplied with anecdotes for the rest of his life. We went from there to the life and times of Ralph and Alma. It was all a delight and we enjoyed it, and soon Kate, being Kate, had adopted little Betsy in absentia, and small gifts and treats went out each day. It had been my intention when we arrived at the Eden to work there, at a desk, while Kate enjoyed a morning of shopping, but it soon became apparent that we weren't going to have any morning life there of our own, but rather the life of Alma, Ralph, and Betsy, and by the time the daily episode had been completed, whatever I might have had to say of my own had vanished from my head.

I approached the manager of the hotel. Not, I hasten to say, in protest of Alma. Almas are rare in the world, and they grow rarer, and we intended to cherish her, but what I wanted to know of Mr. Pickwick was whether he might have some unoccupied space in the reaches of the hotel that I might rent. I wasn't ever quite sure if the manager's name was actually Mr. Pickwick. It sounded something like Pickwick, and he looked like Mr. Pickwick, but he lived in such a frenzy of calamities that I think I would have had to throw him to the floor and sit on his stomach to get him to tell me if I called him by his right name. He was really too busy to care. The Hotel Eden had been built, as I have said, in the vintage days of hotel building in New York, but it was, alas, growing older, and it needed constant care. The veins and arteries of its pipes and heating ducts were subject to hemorrhage, the boilers of the furnace struggled manfully against collapse,

53

the electrical wiring was subject to nervous exhaustion, telephones became hysterical, and coupled with all of this was the burden of the age in which we lived, when no man wanted to do an honest day's work, when you couldn't find anyone who knew anything, when the unions sat in the seat of power and weighed the time of their men against the financial deficit of the hotel, trying always in their cupidity to tread that narrow line between getting every penny the traffic would bear and forcing the hotel to close its doors. Mr. Pickwick was short and round and fat and blurred. He was in constant flight. His best device was to disappear into an automatic elevator, hoping the door would close in the face of his pursuers, but even at best that was momentary respite, for no matter what button he pushed the door was sure to open on Mrs. Selig of 9A, whose sink was stopped up, or Mrs. Golden of 11B, who had just been on her way to see him to report that 11C had smuggled in a dog, and the barking had kept her awake all night.

I learned all of these things because I lay in wait each morning for Mr. Pickwick, and went with him on his rounds, attaching myself to him like a limpet, hoping to snatch a moment of his time like a crumb dropped from a table. Miss Esterhazy at the hotel switchboard, who had been in her little office at the hotel for so long that she blinked when exposed to light, was threatening, again, to quit. The new desk clerk, Mr. Clark, was rude to her and she didn't intend to take it. Mr. Clark was rude to everyone, including Mr. Pickwick and all of the guests, but trained hotel clerks were in short supply. Mr. Pickwick edged himself into Miss Esterhazy's tiny little office. He told her how much he needed her. He knew how sensitive she was. He held her hand. He pleaded with her to stay. Tears came to their eyes as they looked at each other, remembering the anguish of the years they had suffered together at the Eden, their tender union interrupted only when a light flashed on the switchboard in front of her, and Miss Esterhazy would turn to rasp "Hotel Eden!" or "The office!" into the mouthpiece in front of her, in a voice that would have blighted wheat.

At last, persecuted beyond endurance by my unsolicited attention, Mr. Pickwick came up with a solution to my problem. On a gray and blustery morning he took me to the top floor of the hotel, and down a long corridor, half-lit, to an apartment which was not rented because it needed to be redecorated, and funds for that project were not in the budget this year. We walked through the empty rooms, the soot of New York powdering under our shoes. The window of the empty bedroom looked out upon an empty sky, free at that height from buildings. I seized the opportunity. For a small fee Mr. Pickwick gave me a key. With the help of Joe, who wrangled baggage downstairs, we moved a desk into the empty room, and a chair, and I was in business.

It was a lonely aerie. It was a good place to work. The only sounds were the sounds of the steam in the radiators, the distant sirens of the city, the wind against the building, and now and again the sound of another key being put into the lock at the front door, and stealthy steps across the foyer. One other soul possessed a key to my fortress, as Mr. Pickwick had explained at the beginning. This was Miss Hartington, an English spinster lady. The refrigerator in Miss Hartington's apartment had ceased to function and until it could be replaced Miss Hartington had been given permission to use the empty refrigerator in the empty apartment as a place to store her yogurt.

Our life fell into a pleasant routine at the Hotel Eden. At half-past seven or so we were wakened by the jousting garbage men in the lists of the street below. We would raise the vene-

55

tian blinds to look out over the sooty chimney pots of our pseudo-Paris at the sky of New York. As the winter deepened, the scene took on a Japanese effect, with ventilator fans or television aerials outlined against the snow on rooftops as if they were objects which had been selected that morning for our meditation. We felt a childlike delight in our little wintry city nest, warmed by steam heat from the laboring and aged boilers, serenaded by sirens, cut off from the problems of maintenance of a house.

As we sat at breakfast, Alma would come in, all fresh towels and linens, with her newest chapter in the daily soap opera. "Guess what Betsy said last night!" she would cry. "What?" we would ask, turning our morning faces toward Alma. "Well, she's been sort of puzzled ever since Christmas," Alma said. "So, finally, last night, she said, 'If Santy Claus lives up at the North Pole, why do we wait down here for him to come to us? Why don't we go up there to live with him?' "

Our laughter was the cue for my departure. I stood up, brushing myself with my napkin. I brushed Kate with a hasty kiss, just as any commuter might. I went out into the hall and the door closed behind me. I rang for the elevator and went up to my work.

A wonderful silence lay there, along with the soot. Wind whistled around the corner of the building and sometimes flurries of snow whirled against the window panes. I closed the inner door of the bedroom, not even to be disturbed by the stealthy, apologetic arrivals and departures of Miss Hartington with her yogurt, but now and again at some indefinable distance I could hear a student at a piano, practicing scales, a pleasant, monochromatic background for thought. And so I worked at the new script of my play, in blissful ignorance of any catastrophe ahead.

Meanwhile, the day of action had begun for Kate. The city

lay there, waiting for her. Most mornings she began with forays to the local markets, for, again as in Paris, most food had to be bought for the day because of the limited facilities for storage. This part of her day she approached not without some misgivings, and in the end these misgivings loomed largely in her experience, and weighed heavily against other factors in her assessment of life in the city. Upon leaving the door of the hotel, if one turned left one had only to cross the street to be in the park, and on that street the old flavor of that part of the city retained its character. But if on leaving the hotel you turned right and walked to the end of the block, you entered a different and more colorful world where Spanish was the language of the day, for the Puerto Ricans had moved like hermit crabs into what had once been the town houses and apartment houses of middle-class propriety.

The hearing of Spanish spoken on the streets did not intimidate Kate. We had lived a year in Mexico. The alien quality brought to the streets did not intimidate her either. We had traveled abroad. She rather enjoyed the difference of it, and sometimes, if Alma was delayed in coming to us, I would see her off at the door of the apartment before I went up to my work. Kate hated hats. I don't think she had more than one or two, for emergency purposes, such as weddings. She wore a winter coat of knitted wool, and loosely at the neck she would tie a scarf of what I think she told me was wool lace, whatever that is, to be drawn up over her head if she felt that to be necessary. She carried with her a string bag which she had brought from Italy, and which she had used for similar expeditions there when we had once tried to keep house in Rome. It was her talisman, I felt. She was like Little Red Riding Hood, setting out, not for Grandmother's house, but first to get the provisions. Everything was an adventure to Kate. She would convey her excitement and her pleasure to me. What would we have for dinner? Was there anything I particularly longed for? Naturally, it had to be something she could prepare with what equipment she had, but since we had augmented this equipment with a small electric oven there was very little we were deprived of, with the exception, I suppose, of grilled meats. Casseroles, braised foods, roasts; often the scents in the hallways outside the door of our apartment seemed a mockery of the purpose of the serving pantry.

What had the serving pantry been intended for? It dated, I think, from the period of prohibition affluence. There had once been a dining room at the Hotel Eden. There was still a dining room, but it was open now only for such catered functions as a wedding reception, or a Bar Mitzvah, when the lobby of the hotel would be filled with smiling people, emotional, happy, sad, moved. But I thought of the occupants of our apartment at the Hotel Eden in its early days as being figures from the cartoons of John Held, Jr., or from the pages of F. Scott Fitzgerald. I could see the couple of that day coming home drunk and happy and a little disorderly from a nearby speakeasy. They would have telephoned for dinner to be sent up from the kitchens of the dining room, and the man who brought it up would have undoubtedly stayed to serve it, keeping it warm in the serving pantry.

Now, not only was the dining room of the hotel closed, there wasn't even any very acceptable restaurant within blocks. So Kate would set off in the morning with her string bag in search of a plump chicken, or a roast, and the changing character of the neighborhood also had its surprising advantages because there were new and exotic vegetables and fruits to please the new palates. Kate was a woman who loved to shop. Heaven would be for her, I think, one long day of shopping. She loved to handle things, to pick out each onion or potato, and she avoided, with stern disapproval, those markets where potatoes and onions came stapled in bags and had to be bought that way. An eggplant or a zucchini, a tomato or an orange pleased her hand. The textures of all foods drew her. Meat had to be tested through its cellophane wrappings by her practiced finger, and she did not hesitate to break the seal of a package of sliced bacon to see if what was revealed to the eye was all the lean of the meat that there was. "They will certainly not object," she said righteously, "unless they are trying to cheat me."

So off she went each morning, joyously, on her quest. Since we had lived in the city when we were young, she knew how to shop there. She knew also, as many people do not know, that the freshest foods, the superior foods, and foods in greatest variety are to be found in the city, and that people in the suburbs or in the country come off second best, except for those periods of summer when local produce is available. In the city we could have special treats. Kate knew where to find venison, or mutton, or the best rabbit. We could have quail, or pheasant. We could have fresh strawberries and asparagus in winter, and garden lettuces presumably grown for kings, since they were never available to us in the country at any time of the year. For much of this Kate had to go to other parts of the city, but for her local shopping, which she did on foot in the morning, she went to the markets where Spanish was spoken. It was colorful, and the food was of good quality, since only one block separated the world of affluence on the park from the barrio of the Puerto Ricans. Beyond the barrio the slums began, the squalor and misery of the life of the poor in the city. The street of the markets was in a way the line of demarcation, the edge of violence.

But both of us, although I did not know this at the time, lived on the edge of the knife, for it was then that Serge Lichtenstein returned to New York. It was then he wanted to see what I had done with the script. It was then that I really got to know the man.

59

CHAPTER FIVE

Our daily routine was now different. In the morning, instead of going to the calm of my sooty aerie, I went to Serge's apartment, for, and I am certain this news will be received without surprise by anyone who has ever worked in the theater, almost nothing that I had done to the script in his absence pleased him.

In the morning he would face me over the long slab of white marble which served as his desk in his apartment overlooking Central Park from the right side. Here, where everything in the apartment was white, he lived alone, temporarily between wives. The furniture was tubular and ascetic, and on the white walls there were a Mondrian, a Klee, and a Jackson Pollack. Everything was clean, spotless, immaculate, unbreakable, and indestructible. If a fountain pen did not work, discard it. The pencil sharpener whirred constantly. And even though it was winter the fan of the air conditioner would be turned on, to cleanse and circulate the immortal air. Serge would never be by death surprised. He would have been up most of the night, talking, either on the telephone or by direct confrontation, arguing and quarreling. "Who needs sleep?" he would ask. "Everybody sleeps too much! We must work!"

Seated behind the marble slab, he would be wearing a dressing gown of soft white wool. His face was pink and cherubic, and in his ancient, ageless eyes the pupils were suspended like moons in a cloudless sky. He had not slept, but he had bathed. He had bathed once, twice, three times during the night. The white bathroom, with his white telephone beside the tub, would be awash with white bath towels. The whole apartment smelled of his favorite bath oil. When he died, as someone said, being careful to say this behind his back, so that death the unmentionable would not be invoked in his presence, it would not be necessary to have him embalmed, so impregnated was he with his special oils. He would be eating something, a bit of fruit, or even a small, rare steak. By not eating when others ate, at conventional times, he convinced himself that he really did not eat at all. Food, like sleep, was unnecessary. "And why do I not lose weight?" he would ask, regarding his large, rosy, bath-soaked hands. "Today I have eaten nothing at all!"

And folding these hands he would look at me, seated across from him, the beatific smile on his steamed, cherubic face. At such moments I felt myself almost liking him, although later I wasn't quite sure if what I had felt was affection, or merely that curious and rather joyous calm in which a hypnotized rabbit sits, waiting to be devoured. One thing I am sure of. During those weeks, nothing else came to exist for me but that marble-slab desk, the eyes and folded hands of Serge Lichtenstein, and the smell of his bath oil.

That was the way things were meant to be. Since Serge did not permit himself to have a personal life, no one else was to be permitted a personal life. With careful scrutiny he would look over the new pages I had brought to him that morning,

61

the work of the day before, and of the sleepless night, in the
sooty little tower that had now come to seem like a prison.

"And this you would have in the second act?" he would
say, finally, looking up. "It is no good. You must do it over.
You must work harder. We must all work harder. You have
only three weeks before rehearsal. Three weeks! What I ask
is very simple." The smiling lips compressed with a hissing
sound on the word simple, in something like controlled but
impatient despair. "People do not act this way," he would
say. "It is not realistic. And it is a cliché. It has all been done
before. It is not funny. It does not work. It is not theater. We
must all work harder."

Usually at this point the telephone would ring, and in time
this became my cue, one that I imposed upon myself, to go
and sit in the bathroom with the used towels. At first I had
sat with him while he talked, since he motioned for me to
wait. "Darling," he might say. For he did have some personal
life, which, like food and sleep, he denied. "Yes, darling. Yes,
yes, darling." When I rose to go and he motioned for me to
stay, I would hear, unwillingly, the woman's voice at the
other end, sometimes in teasing laughter, sometimes tenta-
tive, sometimes in tears. "I have tickets," Serge would say.
"Yes, if you like, we will dress. Dinner? Oh, afterwards. Today I am not eating. Well, all right, yes, the Colony, Cara-
velle, your place? Do you have some yogurt?"

It was when he spoke in anger that I had learned to leave
the room. After I saw it once I could not sit to watch it again,
even if he motioned to ask me to wait, as his face swelled, the
veins in his neck distended, the lips protruded, and rage
spewed forth from him like excrement. That was when I
would go to the bathroom and step around and over the
mountains of damp white towels, and sit on a stool in the
dressing alcove. Even the closed door could not keep out the

squeal of his rising voice, the vomit of invective. "What do I pay you for? You fool! You are at home? What are you doing at home when I pay you to work? I work! I don't sleep! You can do nothing! I must do it all myself! A moron could do it better! You have not called him? Of course he will be angry! Are you afraid? Are you a coward as well as an idiot? Must I wipe my shoes on you to get you to act?"

And so on and on until it was done, and then, after a moment's pause, the coaxing little voice would come. "Professor? Professor? Please come out, Professor. I have finished."

When I went back to face him across the marble-slab desk again he would be calm, his hands folded, smiling his beatific smile. "It bothered you?" he would say. "One must act that way with fools. And of course they tell me I will never have a heart attack. When you lose your temper that way you will never have a heart attack. It is only the others, the ones who keep it bottled up, who die of heart attacks. And now," he would say, "shall we get back to Act Two?"

And at last we were in rehearsal, but I wasn't there. I was always in my little cage at the top of the Hotel Eden, rewriting the work I had rewritten the day before, while the cast labored over the pages that Serge had grudgingly accepted. I had not been asked to help in the casting, or to approve it, which is the playwright's prerogative, but what could I have been expected to know about that? I had gone to the rehearsal hall once, to meet the cast. It had not been an experience to paste into one's memory book, although I could not quite define what had disappointed me about everything. True enough, the rehearsal hall had been dingy and vacant and cold. The actors, two of them quite well known, had seemed smaller in life, as actors usually do. No, it was something about the way Serge had been making them read my lines that had bothered me. If it was supposed to be comedy, why did they have to shout so loudly? Did they have to seem angry, when I had meant them to be entertaining? But again, who was I to know anything about the theater, having worked all of my professional life in solitary confinement? I remembered the shining archangel assistant of Alton Tweed and his talk about pies in the face. Possibly that was the answer. The lines had to be thrown at the customers.

I wasn't permitted much opportunity for surveillance, or for any expression of doubt. I was introduced to the players, and sent back to my tower prison cell. In my innocence and inexperience I did not know that this was a device, the requests for constant rewriting a ploy to keep me away from any interference during rehearsals. Even so, I had lost all sense of proportion and perspective. Sometimes it seemed to me that I could scarcely remember back to the days when Kate and I had lived together in what now seemed such happy tranquillity. It was paradise lost.

But even I knew that all was lost when I sat one morning in a theater to watch the dress rehearsal run-through before the first preview of the play. My suspicions had been right from the beginning. What had been meant to be light and entertaining came down like a lead balloon, as the players screamed and shouted at each other on the stage, turning banter into that sort of invective which was apparently the only sort of comedy exchange known to Serge Lichtenstein.

I was angry when I went backstage afterward, and I was fortified by the whiskies I had drunk at the bar next door between acts.

"Well, we worked," I said to Serge. They were all there, the cast, the technicians, the stage hands, the people I had never seen. "We worked and we worked and we worked until we worked all the fun right out of it. It isn't funny. It doesn't work, and it isn't theater," I said, throwing his words back at him. "But I should have known better, because this is an American play and you wouldn't understand about that."

Serge's face fell. The pink, cherubic blubber sagged. Afterward I was told that I had hurt him. I had hurt his feelings. I had hurt the feelings of Serge Lichtenstein! It was worthy of an epitaph. Which I felt I needed right about then.

"But I have been an American citizen for twenty-five years!" Serge said. "What do you mean that I would not understand an American play?"

The silence around us made him aware, suddenly, that everyone was watching and listening, and he controlled himself. "Ten minutes!" he shouted. "We will have a ten-minute break and then back in your places! We will rehearse all day if that is necessary! We must work and work and work!"

I, of course, was sent back to the Hotel Eden, with instructions for more last-minute rewriting, and there in the lobby I found Kate. She was sitting in one of the high-backed chairs by the elevator, waiting for it, and at her feet was her string bag, full, and a proliferation of smaller bags. Even in my preoccupation I could see that she looked pale, and when she saw me, tears welled up in her eyes.

"What is the matter?" I said, with alarm. "Oh, my dear, what is the matter?"

The automatic elevator returned to the lobby floor just then, and for a moment we were busy trying to hold the door while we got ourselves and the bundles inside. Kate leaned against me, and I held her, tightly, while the elevator went up to our floor. She tried to tell me what had happened. There had been a fight on the street of the markets. She had been on her way home, her shopping finished, when, from

65

the doors of a café as she passed it had come shouting, the terrible, irrational sounds of violence; men had spilled forth all about her before she could run away; there had been knives, fighting, blood on the sidewalk before she could get away.

Safely in our apartment she lay back on the sofa, pale and trembling, while I made her a cup of tea.

"The city has changed," she said. "I've tried to ignore the changes, but I can't. It used to be so innocent when we lived here. So happy and innocent. It isn't innocent any more."

I brought her the cup of tea, and she sipped it while I made a cup for myself, and below us in the streets was the sound of the perpetual sirens.

"They always say you can't go home again," Kate said, "and I suppose that's true, but I never see you any more, and I know I'm not supposed to complain about that, because you are working for the both of us, but I'm so lonely, and I worry about you because you look so tired, and . . ." She put the cup down and reached for her handkerchief, and the tears began again.

I went to her and tried to comfort her. "It will all be over soon," I said. "For better or for worse, it will all be over soon."

Kate pressed her face against me for a moment, and then she drew back and looked up at me and a smile came over her face, like a rainbow after a summer shower.

"Oh, do hand me my string bag," she said. "I've brought you the most beautiful capon you have ever seen!"

It would be more charitable, perhaps, not to mention the opening of the play at all, although even this was not without its element of mystery for the uninitiated. Disastrous as it seemed to me, to the critics it was neither an unqualified failure nor an unqualified success. It was what it was, a Serge Lichtenstein production, neither fish nor fowl. It might run long enough to get back its investment, or it might not. Certainly it did not do very much for the author, whose name, and possibly this was just as well, could hardly be found anywhere, in the programs, or on the placards in the lobby. The players, through their agents, had reached an armed truce about their billing with Serge Lichtenstein, whose name in lights could be seen for two blocks, overwhelming even the name of the play, as well as all of those connected with it. But, if he had ruined it, the reputation of his name might in some part redeem it for his investors. And then he was off, looking for new fields to lay waste.

Back at the Hotel Eden we packed. But tired as we were, disillusioned as we were, we did not pack to go home. A new *folie de grandeur* had seized us, as if we were caught up in a momentum which we could not stop. We were going to Hollywood. We were going at the invitation of Eric Beane, the television producer. I was persuaded to try my hand at that medium. After all, what was the good of any experience, even an unfortunate experience, if you did not use that experience constructively, for gain?

What good, indeed.

CHAPTER SIX

WE had never been to Hollywood, nor to any part of California. We knew very little about it at all. Friends of ours, neighbors, had moved to California two years before because the husband, Alden Bates, was an actor. He had to go where the action was. The Bateses had clung to the East as long as they could. They had always lived there, and they loved it, but Aldy's position grew more precarious as the theater on Broadway was invaded by plays and actors from England, and as the television studios moved most of their production to the West Coast. We had missed Aldy and Pat and the children, and they had missed us, they always said, in the letters that passed back and forth between Kate and Pat. Kate had corresponded with Pat from the Hotel Eden, and Pat wrote there with a request. Aldy was between acting commitments. He needed a rest and a change. He ought to take off for a few weeks. Would we let them come and stay in our house while we were away, so that they might visit with old neighbors and friends? They would, in exchange, be happy to let us have their house in "the valley" anytime.

This letter with its request had come just as we were about

 68

ready to leave New York, but with it also came a letter from Eric Beane, our friend the television producer, with his familiar invitation. Now that I had got my feet wet in the theater, so to speak, why didn't I come out and try my hand at television?

It seemed like an interesting idea. It could be a part of our exploration of other ways of living. Perhaps California was our answer. Perhaps California was our destiny. Of course it did mean clearing out those closets and bureau drawers, but Kate said she didn't mind doing that for the Bateses. It wasn't like renting the house to strangers. And, besides, Pat would have to do the same thing for us. So, separately, three thousand miles apart, closets and bureau drawers were emptied, and then we all took off by plane, crossing somewhere in mid-air, for our exchange visit. Aldy Bates even offered to leave his car at the airport in Los Angeles for us, mailing me a key, but I declined. I was perfectly willing to leave our car at Kennedy Airport for him, and mail him a key, which I did, but he would know what he was doing when he got there, while for us Los Angeles and "the valley" might well have existed on the moon. There are moments even now when I still think that it does. But not for nothing had we listened to all those jokes on television about the Los Angeles freeways. I would prefer to be delivered to the Bateses' house in the mysterious valley first by taxi or hired car, and then start out from there in Aldy's car to explore the surrounding terrain.

It is not easy to be lucid about Los Angeles. Many have tried, but not, I think, with success. If you have been there you will believe it; if you haven't you won't. We arrived at the Los Angeles airport in a slight precipitation, which we would have called rain, but which the natives seemed to prefer to ignore. Later I was told that this had something to do with local pride. It was not supposed to rain in Los Angeles, so when it did many people just pretended that it didn't. In fact a good many of them, if they were driving a car, did not even turn on the windshield wipers, a phenomenon I observed as we drove away from the airport in a taxi.

The driver of the taxi seemed of the same breed as taxi drivers everywhere. He talked a great deal, and he had a rather low opinion of humanity in general. (The meter in the taxicab was not, however, like the meters in the taxicabs we knew. It started off at about ninety cents, and it registered a dollar and a half even before we got out of the airport grounds.)

"The drivers in Los Angeles are terrible," our driver told us. "The roads are slick with oil from the cars because it hardly ever rains, and when it does the roads are as slippery as glass. But do they slow down? Not on your life."

We were doing about sixty miles an hour ourselves as he imparted this bit of information to us, and I would have closed my eyes except that they seemed stuck open with a kind of awful fascination as we shot along a boulevard and zoomed up and onto what was apparently one of the infamous freeways, joining the traffic without a backward glance of caution from any of us, particularly the drive, at about sixty-five miles an hour, and streaked down the road with the bumper of the car ahead of us and the bumper of the car behind us so close that I think it might have been possible just to slip a copy of the AAA Emergency Service Directory in between. Later that evening we heard routinely announced on the television news that because of the rain five people had been killed in two hundred accidents on the freeways. I think that if there were ever two hundred accidents on the highways of New York City in a comparable length of time, someone in authority would send all the children home again, with instructions to start over and to try to do better. Mean-

70

while Kate clutched my hand and I clutched hers. We looked out of our separate windows. We tried not to look ahead.

The view was dispiriting. It may be that there are people who do not react well to semitropical zones. Kate had once said of Florida that she didn't like it because of the Spanish moss, which looked, she said, like the dust curls under unmade beds. My first impression of Los Angeles was that it was mangy. Los Angeles is a city which sits low on the horizon, although there are a few new tall buildings, built presumably in defiance of the geographical fault on which it rests so perilously. These buildings, I was told, were designed to "float," or to roll with the punches, or something, which was somehow not very reassuring, at least to me. Mostly what we had was an impression of bungalows, a city of summer cottages out of season, lonely in the fog, with here and there, apparently planted at random, long rows of palm trees, like soggy feather dusters.

But first and last there were the cars. Later I found that my hand was numb from where I had clutched at Kate, and she had clutched at me, as we sped at the cruising speed of sixty-five miles an hour down long lanes of traffic four abreast, past long lanes of traffic four abreast going in the opposite direction. "When they have an accident in weather like this," our driver said, "a dozen cars or more will all pile up on top of each other."

"I believe it," I said fervently. "Couldn't you perhaps slow down a bit?"

"Oh, that's what causes the accidents," he said, pressing the gas pedal down to the floor.

But at length we turned off the freeway. We drove down through winding lanes, suddenly sylvan, past houses each as distinctive and as beautiful, as unfamiliar and alien to us as if we were in a foreign land. At last we came up the road where the Bateses' house was, and just as we pulled into the driveway the sun came out with a great burst of glory, to cast its blessing on us and the San Fernando Valley. We had made it. We had arrived in the valley and it was as beautiful as paradise. Surely Adam and Eve could not have felt more awed than Kate and I, as hand in hand we stepped from the taxi, and made our way to the house that was to be ours for the next few weeks.

It looked exactly like a stage setting, all of it. The house didn't fit into any known category of architectural style. It was its own reason for being. It was constructed of various materials, of clapboard and stone, of brick and sheets of glass, with rough-split shakes of cedar for its roof, and it sat in its own landscaped bower of tropical greenery and improbable blooms.

We paid the driver the vast tribute the meter had exacted from us. He helped us with our bags, and drove away, and we were alone.

We made our way inside, too assaulted by strangeness to absorb it all. On the counter space in the kitchen, just as in our own kitchen at home, there were liquor bottles set out, and a note from Pat directed us to our cold supper in the refrigerator. Like Alice in Wonderland, we read and drank and ate. It was six o'clock in Los Angeles, but back in New York, as in our own heads, it was nine o'clock in the evening. It had been a long day. When we had finished eating we went, gratefully, to bed.

The next morning I was up and off to tackle the terrifying freeways on my own. In Aldy's convertible with the top down I felt as if I were in a motion picture, as I went to keep a luncheon appointment, made before we had left New York, with Mr. Eric Beane, my friend the television producer.

Eric Beane, from small beginnings on second-hand movie lots, using second-hand actors and scripts, bargain costumes and faces, had erected an empire that was the envy of all, and gold flowed into his coffers in such a pulsing stream that I had been told he was now buying real estate as far afield as the Bad Lands in South Dakota, having already gobbled up everything available in southern California. We had liked Eric Beane when he had come East to pursue me as a writer. He was a charming man. He smiled a great deal. He resembled, as someone had said, a friendly undertaker. He wore conservative suits. He always wore white shirts and dark ties. It was true that he could talk about almost nothing but money, but the effort to divert the conversation to some other subject was such an intellectual exercise that afterward one felt a sort of curious stimulation. He had come to our house that first day in a rented car with a rented driver, and when he arrived he knew down to the last detail the financial structure of the company from which the car operated, how the driver owned it himself, and leased it back to the company, how he was then paid, and paid the company, or the company bought the car and rented it to him, and then he paid them for renting it back, and they gave him his commission, which he then split—but the mind boggles. At any rate, somewhere at the center of this vortex of financial wizardry, spinning about in the centrifuge, was I, who could write stories, and if I could write stories I could write television scripts, and if I wrote television scripts I would be rich. What a very pleasant idea. Along all the roads leading out from Hollywood the bones of writers bleach under the relentless sun, but these writers were not, of course, good writers, such as I. So quoth Eric.

And here I was now, fearfully steering Alden Bates' convertible along the Ventura Freeway from the valley, to the

Hollywood Freeway, which would take me to Beane Studios, the kingdom of Eric Beane. At Beane Studios television serials were filmed, in half-hour segments, from where they went out to flood the world, appearing not only once but again and again and again, much as the early detergents had backed up in streams and sewers with mountainous suds, threatening to engulf us all, until something called low-sudsing was discovered.

There were several low-sudsing series under production at that very time at Beane Studios. There was "Over the Hills and Far Away," the moving series of a family bankrupted by the Civil War, who had packed everything into a mule wagon and gone to Chicago, where a senile multi-millionaire had fallen in love with the oldest daughter and married her, and now all of the family lived on the North Shore in a Normandy Chateau in hilarious episodes, where their simple honesty and virtue showed up the vulgarity and cupidity of the *nouveau riche* about them. "Over the Hills and Far Away" had been running so long on television that it was not really looked at anymore, but people just left their sets turned on to it as a part of the decoration of the room.

There was also a series called "To Heaven with Love," which was about a beautiful, young, spunky nun who was the athletic coach at a boys' orphanage. "To Heaven with Love" was in its second season and Beane Studios thought it would go on forever, just as "Over the Hills and Far Away" did, if they could just count on Mitzi Midgit, the former child star who played the nun. Mitzi wasn't really sick, but she kept complaining of headaches, and sometimes she threw up on the set. They were hoping a little more money would help clear that up.

Then in the realm of fantasy comedy—as opposed to the everyday realism of "Over the Hills and Far Away," and

74

"To Heaven with Love"—there was the series called just "Gumpy," which was about a man who turned into a horse whenever there was a full moon. His wife had known about this little peculiarity at the time of their marriage, and she had learned to live with it, but her problem was to keep this a secret from their neighbors, and especially from Gumpy's boss, a nervous manufacturer of men's underpants, who had a way of coming up with a business crisis at full moon time, and of popping over to see Alice and Gumpy, and who could never understand why Alice was so hung up on that pet horse of hers that sometimes she even brought it into the house.

Also in the works was a new series, as Eric explained to me over the telephone before we had started out. He wasn't quite sure yet whether it would be a science-fiction series, or a teen-age romance series. Perhaps it could be both in one, a science-fiction, teen-age romance series, with adolescent scientists trapped in a space capsule with a very intelligent chimpanzee, who always turned on the closed television circuit which re-layed pictures back to earth every time the two kids even tried to put their arms around each other. Eric was sure I could write for any one of these series.

I could?

Of course I could. Think of the money that was in it. The original script itself didn't pay too much to begin with, maybe three or four thousand dollars, but if it went into reruns it could go into as many as six, with residual payments each time. (Oh, those golden slippers—Oh, those golden slippers!) And of course that didn't include Latin America, and the Mediterranean countries, and Bulgaria and Outer Mongolia. Why there was a writer right there at Beane Studios who made a quarter of a million dollars a year! A quarter of a million dollars a year! Of course he had ulcers, and had had three wives, but that was the penalty of being such a sensitive creative artist.

The Ventura Freeway socks into the Hollywood Freeway with something of the impact of adrenaline being pumped into the bloodstream, and I knew I was there, in the big time. Above me on either side of the road the feather-duster palm trees stood against the airless sky, and the color in that vacuum was a sort of bronze, so that the first legend one has exploded in Hollywood is that people wear dark glasses not because they hope they will be mistaken for movie stars but because, after a while, you simply cannot see. And everywhere all about was a suggestion of the scent of smoke, as if Sodom and Gomorrah were burning on the next lot.

I had been told to leave the freeway at Franklin, which I did, and proceed on Franklin to Wilshire Boulevard, which led me across Hollywood Boulevard and Sunset Boulevard, and no one has ever been able to describe these locations either, the unreality, the sense of rootlessness which pervades them, the silence which lies over them, in this community where there is no communication, where the crowded sidewalks move with people who do not speak, and even the hippies seem merely to be pretending, lost children from farms in Kansas, collecting dust and disappointment. The temperature stood at eighty. There were girls on the street in bare feet. There was a ragbag of shops and theaters and drug stores and paperback book stores and restaurants and bars, with here and there a private house still standing, even looking occupied, as if the owner had made up his mind to stay there until all the nonsense had stopped.

Beane Studios was situated in what seemed to me like a family neighborhood of suburban houses, streets, fireplugs and sidewalks, palms and oleanders. The studio itself was like a little kingdom, an economy-size Graustark. It was surrounded by a cement wall painted blue, and at the entrance was a little gatehouse from which you expected Dopey or Smiley to pop out, or even the shade of the late Walt Disney. The man who did pop out in uniform was all smiles and informality, and you knew that if he knew your first name he would have called you by that. Informality is the very ambience of Hollywood, or at least it is in this presently sleazy day, and I was told that even if one could afford a chauffeur one did not have one, since this would be considered pretension. On the other hand, only God knew what the standards were for simplicity.

When I had given my name and the magic name of Eric Beane I was waved through the barrier into an inner courtyard and with a sweep of hand told that I might park anywhere I liked. It was a heady sense of triumph, to be in the kingdom at the request of the king, and I felt that the world and a quarter of a million dollars a year were practically mine. I parked the car and then I walked down a path bordered with flowers in what surely seemed a stage set, passing great closed sets where red lights gleamed and signs saying DO NOT ENTER were posted, and soon, in a smaller building, a sort of Petit Trianon, I was in the office of Eric Beane.

Here everything was as folksy as Old MacDonald's Farm. The secretary was cheerful and breezy and spoke to me as if we had known each other all of our lives, with such conviction that I wondered if perhaps we had, possibly having been in nursery school together. Eric himself came out of his office immediately, both hands outstretched, all smiles, warmth, love. He had asked Austin Burns to have lunch with us. Burney, as he was called, was the producer of "Over the Hills and Far Away," and Eric was sure I would be crazy about him. I was a bit confused by this development, having assumed that since Eric Beane owned Beane Studios, surely he was the producer of "Over the Hills and Far Away," but since I did not want to pull my finger out of the dike which held back all the flood of my ignorance about television, I said nothing.

Austin Burns was summoned by the friendly secretary in tones that indicated she had gone to nursery school with him also, and in a moment Burney appeared. He was also wearing a dark suit, a white shirt and dark tie, and an expression of profound gloom. Actually he looked like a very good fake El Greco painting of a saint. There was a little dark cloud just over his head which moved with him when he walked, where a halo might have been in more divine circumstances. Burney was not folksy and he did not smile, but he seemed not unfriendly, and perhaps he had just got out of bed that morning on the wrong side. Together, the three of us went to Eric's car, which was not chauffeur-driven. My borrowed car remained safely within the walls of the kingdom while we were away.

I feel certain there must be places in Hollywood to have luncheon at other than the Brown Derby at Hollywood and Vine, but I was never to find out what they were. We went to the Brown Derby where Eric's car was parked for him, and we walked across the sidewalk set with its stars of terrazzo outlined in brass, each bearing in its center the name of some forgotten movie star, now remembered from a world of innocence and youth, where things seemed, in that memory, to have been built on a grander and more generous scale. For a moment one wanted to say: No, I don't want to do this. Let us go back. I prefer to have my memories. But we went in, to be greeted effusively by the headwaiter, and soon we found ourselves seated in a circular leather banquette around a round table, with a physical intimacy one had thought was usually reserved for seduction.

78

I was in the middle. My panic subsided somewhat over a martini. We lunched on sand dabs, whatever they are, and while we lunched we told stories. Burney had written, at one time or another, for every television series in Hollywood. It is said that Alexandre Dumas *père* had a factory for the writing of novels, where many writers were employed. With Burney Burns, Father Dumas could have chucked the whole lot. A torrent of situations poured forth from his gloomy El Greco face. Urged on by Eric Beane, who also wanted to get into the act, he sought by this means to convey to me how the writing for television series was really accomplished. A half-hour script must have, just as the old-fashioned short story was required to have, a beginning and a middle and an end. Unlike the old-fashioned short story, however, it was imperative that in a half-hour television script nothing must happen.

Every journalism freshman knows that in the classical short story a climax must occur in which the lives of the principal characters will be presumably changed forever by some enlightenment, either brought on by outside circumstances, the *deus ex machina* of the Greeks, or preferably, more skillfully, by the interplay of the characters themselves, the revelations that come about by their confrontation. But if this were to happen in an episode of a television series, where would the characters go from there? After all, they had to come back next week, unchanged, so what was wanted was something very different, something called, irreverently, by its critics, *shtick*. Although that unfortunate word was not invoked at the Brown Derby, it hung about us in the air. *Shtick* was skin deep. It was not character in action. It was, well, situation. Situation comedy, which was what television comedy series were, was not a story with a beginning and a middle and an end, it was a situation with a beginning and a middle and an end. It was a learned technique, Eric hastened to assure me.

79

In the beginning you put in a little hook, a something to hold the attention. You developed that. In the end you resolved it.

"Take for example," Burney said, "the script I am working on now. Ma is taken down with a bad cold and Aunt Hildegarde comes to take care of the house for her. While Aunt Hildegarde is there she discovers that an old beau of hers lives in town whose whereabouts she had forgotten. The old beau comes around to spark Aunt Hildegarde. Now Pa worries about this. Why?" This was the problem they had to work out from the basic premise, Burney said, fixing me with his gloomy face, the halo-cloud above his head lowering, so that I feared for rain.

"Do television comedy writers ever laugh?" I asked impulsively, wanting to divert the whole thing from me, Eric's fixed smile on one side, the threat of rain on the other.

Eric laughed at this, but Burney did not. "It is a point of professional pride," Burney said, "that TV comedy writers never laugh. We always say that if you ever saw a comedy writer laugh it would be like a prostitute having an orgasm." Well, that wasn't exactly the way he said it, but since the language seemed as offensive as the simile, I give you my translation.

But nothing could stop the story. Burney seemed to wear blinders as well as his halo of gloom. His was a one-way mind, and if he made a quarter of a million dollars a year I wondered what he did with it to enjoy it. No, Pa in the script was worried for Aunt Hildegarde—well, what if she was a war widow and she had a fortune, and the old beau was after the money? Burney asked.

"Or what if the old beau only thought she had a fortune, and she didn't have any money at all!" Eric said, gleefully jumping into the fray.

"But what if Ma, lying there in bed," Burney said, "knew

80

that the old beau was really a secret agent for the F.B.I., and he was due for a promotion, and would be a good catch for Aunt Hildegarde?"

"Or what if the old beau was pretending to be a secret agent for the F.B.I.?" Eric said. "What if the F.B.I. was really after him, because they thought he was mixed up in that scandal about the contractor who built the school which fell down, because he had used too much sand in the concrete? Wouldn't that be a laugh?"

"What if Aunt Hildegarde went after the real F.B.I. agent," Burney said, "to get him to protect her old beau, because she knew he was innocent, and Pa found them together, and thought she was trying to make up to another man?"

"And Pa would tell this to Ma," Eric said. "And this would make Ma so mad that she would be suddenly cured of her cold, and she would get right up out of bed and send Aunt Hildegarde back home to Possum Junction?"

"But at the depot," Burney said, "while they were waiting for the train, Aunt Hildegarde would explain to Ma that she had just been trying to protect her old beau because she knew he was innocent, but she really didn't give two hoots about either one of the men."

"Because," said Eric, with a rising note of triumph, "there was a rich old bachelor sparking her back in Possum Junction!"

"And she had to get back there to protect her interests," Burney said.

"And then Ma and Aunt Hildegarde would kiss goodbye," Eric said. "And there would be a fadeout of the train going around the bend, with Aunt Hildegarde waving from the window, and that would be it!"

And there you were! Another script! An absolutely flawless script! Full of noise and confusion. Full of sound and fury.

But no one had changed. And nothing—absolutely nothing—had happened! "Over the Hills and Far Away" could go on happily to the next episode. My heart sank with the sand dabs.

"But of course you can do it," Eric said. We were back at the studio. Luncheon was over. Burney had gone on, scurrying away under his cloud of gloom, to urge the actors on, to work on the new script, to read actors for the guest spot in the next show, to call the doctor about his ulcer prescription. Eric was holding my hand in his. "Give it a try," he said. "Just sit down and sketch out an idea. We need you. We need new ideas. I'll get you some scripts to look over. You'll see how easy it is."

"Could I see the sets?" I asked in a small voice.

Could I see the sets? Of course I could see the sets. We were standing in the inner courtyard of Beane Studios and Eric now guided me toward the center of the complex of buildings. We passed a building marked "Dispensary." We passed buildings, like cottages, marked "Dressing Rooms." We passed mysterious and complex equipment, and large metal boxes bearing identification in code. We passed a chimpanzee and his keeper. Eric swept his arms out in a wide, embracing gesture. "It always gives me a thrill," he said, "to think of all the pleasure that has gone to so many millions of people from these buildings."

We had now reached a door marked "Do Not Enter," and opening it, we entered. We were in a world of tangled darkness. Ropes, wires, cables were everywhere, overhead and underfoot. "Please be careful," Eric said, guiding me by one elbow. In the soaring darkness above us there were cranes and the flats of sets not in use, and lights, lit and unlit. At the center of this dark confusion, glowing like a jewel, or a casket of jewels, or, as it actually was, a stage set, was a lighted set from "Over the Hills and Far Away," and on this set they were doing a scene. What a sense of privilege came to me, of excitement and pleasure. Here I was, in the heart of this magical world, which few outsiders ever penetrated.

Stumbling over cables, I was guided by Eric to one of those canvas chairs which have always been associated with stage sets in Hollywood, and there I found myself seated like a satrap, waiting to be entertained.

It was not entertaining. The scene was the grand entrance hall of the multi-millionaire's house in Chicago. Ma was to come downstairs and open the front door and find a delivery boy there with a bouquet of flowers, and she was to say, "For me?" with disbelief, and apparently this simple scene brought to a head all of the neurotic compulsion for perfection of the entire assemblage. The scene was done not once, not twice, but ad infinitum. In the towering shadows about us I could now begin to make out the vast number of people involved in the project. There were men at cameras, with men beside the men at cameras to tell them what to do. There were directors and assistant directors, and men and women holding books or sheets of paper, and electricians and technicians and assistant technicians, clustered in hivelike groups under a great sibilant buzzing of muted conversation, until a voice would say, "Silence. Let's do it again. Roll it. Number forty-three." And silence would fall on the multitudes, and Ma would come running down the stairs again, brushing a wisp of gray hair back from her made-up face, and open the door, and say, "For me?" and then the same voice would say, "Cut!" And it would have to be done all over again. With less feeling. With more feeling. With the head turned this way or that. With the words spoken from behind the door, or through the door, or under the door.

"Shall we go?" whispered Eric. We got up quietly in the

shadows and stole away. "Does it always go on like this?" I whispered back. "Oh, yes," said Eric. "They come at about seven in the morning, to be made up, and they usually work till half-past six or seven every evening. They want enough takes to have a choice when they put the show together. It takes all week to make a half-hour show."

Out from that building we went, into the glare of sunlight, and into the tangled darkness of another building beside it. Here "To Heaven with Love" was being done. The set, that jewel of light in the disordered shadows, was that of a sandlot baseball diamond, amazingly fake with its artificial grass under the lights. In one corner of the set several young boy actors in baseball suits, with make-up and dirt artfully applied to their faces, cowered nervously. Mitzi Midgit, in her nun's habit, was sobbing. Someone, a man, the director, the producer, someone, with arms around her as she stood at second base, was trying to comfort her. "But I can't do it!" Mitzi wailed. "I can't! I've tried and I've tried, but I just can't say it!"

"But of course you can say it, my dear," her comforter said, holding her. "Of course you can. We'll just take a little rest, and then we'll start over again. From the top."

"Oooo!" gasped Mitzi, clasping her hand to her mouth. "Oooo!" And as if on cue, some waiting minion dashed from the shadows with an enameled basin. Mitzi Midgit threw up.

"Shall we go on?" Eric whispered, smiling his eternal smile. We stole away in the darkness, and passing through the outer glare once more, we went into a third building, where a scene from an episode for "Gumpy" was being filmed. Here, under the beautiful lights, Mrs. Gumpy was speaking to Gumpy in his metamorphosis as a horse. She was saying one line to the impassive horse, an addict, obviously, long hooked on Miltown. "But dear," Mrs. Gumpy said, "you told me the full moon was next week."

Again we were witness to the incredible patience, the painstaking struggle for perfection of artistry, the attention to detail, to nuance, to lighting and grouping, which surely would have been the envy of the great Stanislavsky himself, as Mrs. Gumpy said, after each injunction to roll it, "But dear, you told me the full moon was next *week!*" "But *dear,* you told me the full moon was *next* week!" "*But* dear, *you* told me the full moon was next week!" "But dear, you *told* me . . ."

"Shall we go?" whispered Eric, smiling at my elbow.

Shall we go? "I can hardly tear myself away," I whispered back. But we stole away, and went outside to stand under the flat sunlight, beside my borrowed car, while Eric importuned me.

"Of course you can do it," he said again. He handed me the scripts some nameless and faceless lackey had brought to him, which he had arranged to have brought to him, presumably, at some point in our tour of the sets. I took them and saw that they were copies of former episodes in "Over the Hills and Far Away." Such imaginative empathy, I thought to myself, for over the sand dabs, when pressed as to which of the properties I might like to contribute to (not whether I would like to write for any of them, but, the more subtle approach, which one?) I had replied, somewhat apologetically, that I didn't think I knew very much about nuns, especially nuns who served orphan boys as athletic coaches; or about men who turned into horses at the time of the full moon; or even about teen-age scientists who flew about with chimpanzees in space capsules. So here I was, holding the scripts of "Over the Hills and Far Away," or as I soon learned to call it, as everyone else called it, just "Hills."

"Try an idea," Eric said. "Just a story line. A couple of pages will do it."

I drove away thoughtfully, through the gate, past the gatehouse where the smiling gatekeeper waved me on as if I were already a member of the confraternity of first-namers, being reminded by his smile of the intensity which I had left behind, where, in a studio devoted entirely to comedy and to the bringing of laughter to others, even if it came in cans, so devoted were all concerned to the exacting demands of their craft, and so absorbed, that I had heard no one laugh, nor even seen anyone smile, with the exception of Eric Beane.

Past Wilshire Boulevard I went, and on to Hollywood Boulevard, to make my way to the office of Manners-Classical. At Manners-Classical was Burton Parker, the West Coast representative of Bert Thompson, with whom I had made an appointment before going to Beane Studios. I could see it from afar, as I approached, the building which housed Manners-Classical, for it was built as a replica of the Chateau at Blois, but with two outside staircases instead of one. I tried to dismiss the feeling of awe which came over me as I parked the car in its bowels, and took an elevator to Burton Parker's office. I reminded myself that the name of the firm was not self-exclamatory, but was merely the result of a merger between a Mr. Manners, and an agency formerly called Classical Properties, but the fortuitous coupling of names struck me with that sense of ultimate authority, which, indeed, it enjoyed in the industry. If Manners-Classical was not Mount Olympus where the gods resided, it was at least there that the business managers of the gods lived and had their place of being, and any thunderbolts that were launched came from that pad. Even the switchboard operator knew that. When one telephoned, that presiding deity did not answer with anything so prosaic as "Hello," or even the name of the company;

instead, she breathed its initials, "M-C," into the mouthpiece in front of her, as if she were a sex goddess expiring in a last moment of ecstasy.

The outer office, furnished, like a boudoir, in pink and gray, with chairs and sofas in Louis XVI, contributed to this image of sensual hedonism, but in his matter-of-fact office inside, Burton Parker was the sort of young man with whom you might expect to discuss pork futures in an office on LaSalle Street in Chicago.

"I have an idea you are going to go ahead and try this," he said, "whatever I might say."

I sat opposite him and looked at him across his desk. "But it all seems so pleasant," I said. "I had always thought that Hollywood would be so intimidating." All my reservations had taken wing and flown away, my apprehensions, the memory, over the years, of the tales of writers corrupted, destroyed, creatively ruined by Hollywood. How could anyone be corrupted or destroyed by anything so charming and so mindless?

"You are a writer," Burton Parker said. "These men are not writers. They are carpenters and hacks. They put things together."

"Well, it wouldn't have to be forever," I said, thinking about the quarter of a million dollars.

"You will learn about Hollywood as Candide learned about the world," he said. I wanted to point out to him that he seemed rather young to be playing Dr. Pangloss to my Candide, but in Hollywood I was feeling younger by the moment, so I said nothing.

We regarded each other for a moment, and finally Burton Parker shrugged and threw up his hands. "You want to try it," he said. "I don't think anything I say will influence you." The scene had a strange quality of *déjà vu*, as if I were a boy again, proposing a course of action that was frowned upon by a stern but indulgent father. I half expected him to say, Don't come running back to me when you get hurt. So I said that, out loud.

"You mean," I said, "Don't come running back to you when I get hurt?"

Parker laughed. "I'll do what I can," he said. "I do think, though, that you ought to go ahead on this just on an informal basis. Since you think Eric Beane is your friend, just do a story idea for him, and then if he is interested I will discuss terms with him."

"You sound sort of doubtful about Eric Beane," I said. "Isn't he a man you can trust?"

"You can trust all of them," Parker said. "Up to a point."

On that note we parted.

I drove back to the valley. I was more confident now on the freeway. Fantasy had taken me by the hand. I was a writer in Hollywood, discussing scripts with a producer and with an agent. I who had always written stories was now in a story. Even Alden Bates's car seemed cued in. We scooted along at sixty-five, bumper to bumper unafraid, out the Hollywood Freeway, into the Ventura Freeway, off at the proper exit, and up and around through the flowered lanes to the little dream house in its semitropical setting.

A transformation had also taken place in Kate. She had been able to get in touch with an old classmate from college, who had come to her rescue to take her shopping. She had gone first to buy something suitable to wear in her new life, and now she was in yellow linen trousers, with a fitted jersey or something on top. There were sandals on her bare feet, and she had gathered her hair up and pinned it on top of her head. She was arranging cut freesia in a low bowl. She looked like Ginger Rogers in a comeback, and although I didn't feel quite like Fred Astaire I said nothing, because I also felt I

88

might just make it, any day now. We kissed, rather theatrically.

"How did things go?" Kate asked.

"Just great," I said. "I'm going to try a story idea for Eric Beane. He's given me some scripts to look over."

"That's marvelous!" Kate said.

"I'll put the scripts in Aldy's study before I forget," I said, "and then I'll freshen up a bit for dinner. What is for dinner?" I asked.

"It's practically ready," Kate said. "I thought we'd have just a simple, cold supper tonight. We're having caviar soup, Crab Louis, hearts of palm with hollandaise, and I found some wonderful red lettuce for salad."

"Red lettuce?" I said.

"Oh, you wouldn't believe the markets out here," Kate said. "They're simply fantastic! You wouldn't believe it!"

"I do believe," I said fervently. "I do believe."

We had a cocktail on the terrace at the back of the house, beside the swimming pool, to watch the sun set over the palm trees. It seemed to take a very long time to set, much longer than it took at home, with all sorts of extravagant color effects in the sky, great banners of purple and magenta which would have seemed merely vulgar in a painting, and while it made up its mind to set, we talked about Hollywood.

"I can't understand why people knock it," I said. I had changed into something more appropriate too. I had put on tennis sneakers and slacks and a sport shirt open at the throat, and I was wearing a blue linen jacket which I had bought the previous year, but which I had never had the courage to wear before. And, naturally, because of the glare and the setting sun, we were both wearing dark glasses.

"I can't either," Kate said. "I think it is all perfectly beautiful. Andrea drove me around today to see some of the places.

89

We drove through Beverly Hills, and I can't tell you how beautiful it is."

"Of course, if I get involved in television," I said, taking a sip from my cocktail, "we would have to move out here."

We stared at each other, tentatively, through our dark glasses, trying on the words for size.

"You mean we might have to sell the house," Kate said.

"Possibly," I said.

"It would be a whole new life, wouldn't it?" Kate said.

"Yes, it would," I said.

We were silent for a moment again, staring blankly with our shielded eyes at the vari-colored sky.

"Everything seems so pleasant out here," Kate said.

"And every one seems so pleasant," I said.

"What we really ought to do," Kate said, thoughtfully, "is to call on all the people we know out here, just to see where we might want to live. That is, if we do have to move out here."

"That's a very good idea," I said, standing up. "I think I'll have another drink."

"I think I'll have one, too," Kate said, holding out her glass.

In the morning I was up early and at the desk in Aldy's study, a pleasant room which looked out on a small garden, Japanese style, with a dwarf pine tree in an arrangement of rocks and pebbles. It seemed appropriate for my thoughts. A learned technique, I said to myself, facing my portable typewriter. A learned technique, as opposed to inspiration, or the creative impulse. What was wanted was a situation. A situation with a beginning, a middle, and an end. A hook, at the beginning, to get the viewer into the story. You developed it. You resolved it.

Well, I could do it. I could do it. The night before I had

sat up to read the six scripts which Eric had given to me, former episodes in "Hills." It had been an instructive experience. I found that as I finished one script and went on to the next, the first one vanished completely from my mind. When I had finished reading all six, I could remember none of them, and a curious seizure of yawning had come over me, compulsively, so that I feared for my jaws, which seemed to threaten to become unhinged. I brewed coffee and read all of them again. They all seemed completely new and somehow invisible, so that I found myself distracted by such irrelevancies as the texture of the paper, which seemed to show through more than it did in the average typescript, and in the end I could remember none of them again.

The major difficulty seemed to be that all of the characters were alike, or possibly even the same character. They were endowed with individual names, but they all talked in the same way, a sort of folkish esperanto, the women as well as the men, and they were given to peculiar locutions, which seemed not to be regional, at least not in any sense that I knew of, but to represent some great universality of booboc-racy.

Well, I could do it. I would do it. I would sit there every day at that desk until I learned. I ended up by making a chart of the regular characters in the series, showing their relationships to each other, and then writing each of their names on a slip of paper and pinning these slips of paper with thumbtacks to the bulletin board over the desk, where I could move them about like checkers in some game on the top of a cracker barrel in a back-country general store.

Kate, meanwhile, was on the telephone. We did not know many people in the neighborhoods of Hollywood, but we did know a few, and they were generous, and hospitable, and free with invitations.

We had brunch on a Sunday with the Fosters, on the top of a mountain in Topanga Canyon, which was supposed to be the new "in" place for people in the industry because it was so far out, but getting up to it, and down from it again, on a hairpin road without guardrails, after vodka Bloody Marys, made me feel that we wouldn't be in too long before we were out, so we abandoned the idea of living in Topanga Canyon, on my quarter of a million dollars a year.

We had dinner with the Danners in Beverly Hills, but I felt you had to have something more solid under you than just a yearly income of a quarter of a million dollars to live in Beverly Hills. Betsy Danner had a few oil wells in Texas, which I feel should be mandatory for the wife of any writer, but Beverly Hills scared us, quite a lot. The whole place seemed to be paved with that new material which can be used either indoors or out, and comes dyed to look like grass, or sidewalks, or even street paving. You felt that the streets were gone over with a vacuum cleaner at night, after everyone had gone to bed, and the houses were gone over with a feather duster. Beverly Hills did not seem to sit out in the open, under the sky, but to exist under some vast dome on a stage, and guards, called policemen, went around in cars to ask the names and purposes of any persons who were foolish enough to walk on its sidewalks.

Kate's old school chum, Andrea, lived on a hilltop in Brentwood, with a really spectacular view, but her property kept growing smaller because chunks of it had a way of falling off now and then and rolling down into the valley. Andrea kept planting honeysuckle, or Virginia creeper, or something, in an effort to hold it all together, but just when she got that going fairly well, a brush fire might flash down from the hills. Andrea could save her house by standing on the roof with a hose, keeping the shakes wet down, but the fire always got the Virginia creeper. I didn't think I would ever sleep very well there.

Finally we sort of tentatively decided that when the time came we would choose between Santa Monica or Pacific Palisades. In Santa Monica it was possible to live on the ocean front, and that had its drawbacks with the glare and the morning fog, but there was also the splendor of the sea. In Pacific Palisades there were winding roads under eucalyptus trees, and beautiful, hidden retreats, where congenial people had built houses just out of sight of each other, but near enough to visit.

And what of our own Cliffside, back home there on the dreary old East Coast, where we had lived for all of our married life, and knew everyone there as well as we knew ourselves? Why, that was the past. That was the shabby, gray old past, and we turned our backs on it without a second thought, as we tooled about in the Bateses' convertible, in our dark glasses and our bright new clothes, to see our bright new friends.

Meanwhile, I worked on that first quarter of a million. When I had done two story outlines I decided I had the courage to show one, and I called Eric, and we made a date for lunch. There were just the two of us this time, and we sat in the seductive intimacy of a round table at the Brown Derby and told stories. We were children together.

"I never knew work could be such pleasure," I told the smiling Eric.

We had the pages of the story idea spread out before us on the table while we ate, and Eric would pick up one or the other of them at random, and study them, and come up with new ideas. "I think it's great," he said. "I've never known any writer to grasp the technique so quickly. I think you could show this story outline just as it is, without any changes. Perhaps that might be best," he said. "It's up to you."

He puzzled me when he spoke of *showing* the story outline, because I assumed that by bringing it to him, who owned Beane Studios, that I *was* showing the story outline.

Eric was very patient and kind with me. My ignorance was understandable. After all, most of my life had been spent in an ivory tower, where I wrote stories and lowered them in a basket from a window, and then pulled the basket back up with a check inside. It would be more "tactful" to send the story outline first to Austin Burns, because Burney was, after all, the producer of "Hills."

"But I thought you were the producer of 'Hills'," I said.

Eric smiled benignly and patiently. "I am the *executive* producer," he said. "I am the executive producer of all the shows at the studio, but each show has its *own* producer."

I thought I understood that. It seemed a little like Chinese boxes, but I suppose it was merely a matter of business organization. Possibly for tax purposes. Almost everything in Hollywood was designed with an eye for tax purposes. But of course I would send the story outline first to Burney. I certainly wouldn't want to offend him, or make him feel that he had been bypassed, just because Eric and I hit it off so well. I wouldn't want him to be jealous. But I did think I would rework the story outline first, to put in those ideas we had discussed. It had all been such a pleasure. I could see how delicious the whole thing was going to be.

Actually, I felt a little reluctant to part with the story outline and move into the next category of success. We were having such a good time. We had now definitely decided that when the time came we would settle ourselves in Pacific Palisades. Kate had even written a letter—to help me, as she sometimes did, in mundane business affairs, so that my precious creative time would be wholly free—to a friend of ours at home, a real estate agent, to tell her that we had decided to put our house on the market, and to sound out what prospects there were.

Our confusion and uncertainty of the past seemed almost ridiculous now. Kate had also written to Cam, and he had replied, thoughtfully, and at some length, that while he would miss the old house, the "old homestead," as he had once called it, certainly the practical thing to do was to sell it. It was an old house. It would need constant maintenance. To rent it at such a distance also seemed impractical. He agreed. Of course we must sell it. We had had a happy life there, and nothing could ever take the memory of those years from us.

We liked that. We would settle for that. And think what a privilege it was, at our time of life, to be starting a new life! We felt rejuvenated, young again. Kate augmented her supply of trousers with others, for wear at home, and even for going out to see friends. I liked it. Very few women have the figure for pants, but Kate did. She took to wearing her hair a new way, too, cut shorter and curled in loose curls all over her head. She looked like a pretty tomboy as she worked in the Bateses' garden. "I can hardly wait to have our own garden," she said. "But I'll have to start learning all over again. There are so many varieties of things in California that I know nothing about."

We had been helped in our decision to settle in Pacific Palisades because we had new friends there, the Andersons, whom we had met at mutual friends'. Kate and Molly Anderson had taken to each other, from their love of gardening, I think, and we went often to the Andersons' house in the late afternoon for a drink. Hal Anderson was also a writer of television comedy, but I didn't tell him of my involvement with

95

Eric Beane because I wanted to wait until it was all arranged and spring it on him as a surprise. The Andersons had a pretty house of fieldstone and redwood which spanned a small ravine, with a brook flowing beneath. Trees rose in and around and through the house, which was decorated with Oriental objects of art and three small children, and I felt certain that Hal must also be one of the quarter-of-a-million-dollars-a-year men. He never smiled, which seemed to prove that point, and I never heard him laugh, but I was careful not to draw attention to that since I didn't want to hear again, particularly, that simile of a writer of comedy laughing.

Hal's life was divided between three interests. When he wasn't writing, in his little cell-like studio detached from the house, and when he wasn't in his bar drinking, he was out at a community tennis court, with a fierce contingent of neighbors, to release, as he said, his hostilities and aggressions. I went there once as a spectator, and I decided that when we became neighbors I would decline any invitations to tennis. I have always felt that when my time comes I will be as ready to go as the next man, but I didn't think I wanted to go that way.

In due course I finished the revisions on the story outline for "Hills," and with commendable pride I put it in an envelope and mailed it off to Mr. Austin Burns, Producer, "Over the Hills and Far Away," Beane Studios, Hollywood, California. I then sat back to wait.

I didn't have to wait long. The telephone rang the next afternoon. I heard it in the dressing room off of our bedroom, where I was standing at a mirror, rubbing into my hair a preparation I had bought that morning at the drug store, which promised to darken your hair "imperceptibly," so that even your best friends wouldn't notice when your graying locks had vanished, and you were restored to your old ravishing self. I tried to wipe the goo off my hands with a towel as I went to the telephone.

It was Austin Burns. "I started to write a letter to you," he said, when he had identified himself, "but then I decided I could better say to you what I have to say over the telephone."

"Good," I said.

"The material is quite unsuitable," he said.

"It's what?" I said. I sat down on the little chair next to the telephone table. I knew that Burney wasn't smiling, since he never did, and now I stopped smiling.

"It's quite unsuitable," he said.

"It is?" I said. "In what way?"

"It is contrived and artificial and lacking in structure," he said. "It really wouldn't do."

A metamorphosis had taken place in our El Greco. There was a cold arrogance in his voice which had not been there that day over luncheon at the Brown Derby, and the deliberate offense of his words, from the master artificer of the contrived and artificial, so angered me that I had to speak very slowly. All the blood left my head, but I felt all would go well if Burney just kept on saying things that I could repeat.

"It wouldn't do," I said.

"It is possible, of course," he said, "that you just can't write for television."

"Possible," I said.

"After all," he said, "you have spent most of your life in another field."

"Another field," I said.

"Of course," he said, "if you really do want to try your hand at script writing seriously, I could give you an assignment."

"An assignment?" I said, varying the routine a bit. He

wasn't near enough for me to attempt assault, so I began to feel a little more in control of myself.

"Well, you see," he said, "what you have sent me really isn't anything. I don't know if you would care to try again, since it may not be work you can do, but if you would like to try some simple assignment, some story with a little sense in it, I could send you an agreement form."

"What is an agreement form?" I asked.

"It would authorize you to attempt a story line for me," he said. "A story idea. A story idea must have a beginning and a middle and an end, with a hook, you know, at the beginning."

"It seems to me I've heard that somewhere before," I said.

"Of course if you accepted an assignment," he said, "you would be paid."

"I would?" I said. "How very nice. How much would I be paid."

"The Guild minimum," he said. "Three hundred dollars."

"I hope you will allow me to think that over," I said, and I replaced the telephone, very gently, in its cradle.

I don't remember exactly how I got there, and my not remembering may be one of the many contributing causes to the great number of accidents on the Hollywood Freeway, but the next thing I knew I was standing in the office of Burton Parker at Manners-Classical.

"I told you that you would learn about Hollywood," Parker said, "as Candide learned about the world."

I said aloud what I had thought earlier, that he seemed to be rather young to be playing Dr. Pangloss, "and besides," I added, "I think I find it inexcusable to be still playing Candide at my age."

"Then I will be Virgil to your Dante," Parker said, "and

show you the lower depths of hell. But I think you had better sit down," he said. "You look quite white." He took a bottle of scotch from a lower drawer of his desk and poured a stiff dollop into a glass and handed it to me. I drank it and sat down.

"Hollywood is the cruelest place in the world," he said.

"But you'll have to start at the beginning again and tell me what happened," I said. "I didn't even know I had been stabbed in the back until I saw the blood running over my shoes. Why did Eric Beane encourage me to get into this?"

"Because he would really like to see you do it, I suppose," Parker said. "You told me he was your friend. He could throw you into the pool, but you have to learn to sink or swim on your own."

"With a friend like that who needs enemies," I said, grateful to whoever it was who had coined that old chestnut.

"Austin Burns is protected by a contract," Parker went on. "He has a literary agent, he has lawyers, he is a member of the Writers Guild. As long as he holds that contract he will decide who will write the scripts for that show. You are an outsider. You are a threat. All of the writing for these television series is done by about thirty men. There are five of them for every available job. They all know each other. They will fight among themselves, but they will close ranks if threatened. This is their turf. They will guard it with their blood. Do you think they will lie down and let someone come in and steal their swimming pools?"

"Then why did he offer me this so-called assignment?" I asked.

"Probably just to save face. For everyone. You were introduced as Eric Beane's friend."

"And Eric Beane has nothing to say about any of this?"

"Not as long as Austin Burns's contract runs," Parker said.

"In the industry there is only one value. It is money. You don't have to like another man. You don't have to care whether he likes you. You don't even have to speak to each other. As long as the ratings hold."

"What is all this talk about the money to be made in writing for television?" I asked. "What has three hundred dollars got to do with a quarter of a million dollars a year?" I hated the sound of my voice as I spoke, and the words that I said, seeing, with a sense of sick revelation, that I had been lured into this swamp, and undone by simple greed. What sort of man had I become?

"That's where you have to start," Parker said. "And that's where Eric Beane hopes you will start. But it's worse even than you know, because you wouldn't even get any farther than that, not on this go around. Burney and his buddies would see to that. But even if they did buy the story idea, which they wouldn't, then you would have to do a step-out."

"A what?" I said.

"A step-out," Parker said. "That's when you begin to write the dialogue. It's when you start to flesh out the outline which you did in the beginning. Look," Parker said, standing over me. "This isn't writing. This is the carpentry I spoke about. This is hack work. I've known Austin Burns for a long time. He is a very competent hack. He works very hard. And it is hard work. Do you want to learn how to grind out a thirty-page script, week after week, to please a lot of foolish sponsors and empty-headed actors and actresses and all the mindless people in the agencies? Eric Beane hopes you will. Austin Burns and the others like him will die or burn out some day, and Eric likes to have reserve pitchers warming up in the bull pen. Why in two or three or maybe four years you might have your foot in the door and even begin to make a little money."

Years before, when I had first begun to write, I had been

faced with a similar decision. Even before television there were decisions of that kind to be made. I had learned then, at the very beginning, that it took just as much hard work and effort to learn to be a hack as it did to learn to be an honest writer. I had made a decision then to go my own way, and while a suspicion had been growing in me of late that I might never write the sequel to *War and Peace,* I knew, with greater certainty, that I didn't want to spend the rest of my life trying to write *shtick*. I would never make a quarter of a million dollars a year, because I didn't want it that much.

I might have gone back to the valley in the same state of somnambulistic shock in which I had left it but for the fortunate accident of seeing Miss Sex Goddess in the outer offices of Manners-Classical as I was leaving. She was so famous that I knew I would remember her name when I got my mind back, but it did not come to me then. She was a tall, tawny beauty, long-limbed, and someone had forgotten to tell her that she was not dressed when she left the house. She was clad in what appeared to be two knitted potholders, one in front and one in back, suspended over her shoulders by black shoe laces, and when she stood and stooped over to stub out a cigarette in an ashtray I was returned to consciousness with a gratifying jolt.

Kate was working out in the garden when I went back to her, and I mixed a couple of drinks for us and carried them outside. We were well into our last week in the Bateses' house, and Kate was busy with the planting and the flowers because, as she said, she wanted everything to look nice for them when they got back. We had decided to move into a hotel until we found just the house we wanted in Pacific Palisades. Oh, yes, we would. I handed her a drink and asked her to sit down and then I told her the whole sorry tale.

101

As I talked I remembered what I had once read of Robert Clive's impression when he had first seen India, before he had conquered it. It had seemed to him so corrupt, so ready to fall, so burstingly overripe in the sun that he knew it could be had by the first hand that reached out for it. Television seemed not unlike that to me, at least that part of it that passed as entertainment. Someday someone would come along and take all the swimming pools away and show everyone what could really be done.

"Well, it was fun while it lasted," Kate said, when I had finished. "Now let's be sensible and go home." She got up and went toward the house. "And if you don't mind," she called back, "I think I'll take off these pants. They get so uncomfortable after a while."

The telephone rang when she had gone, and I went into the study to pick it up. It was Eric Beane.

"I've just heard that Burney didn't like the story idea," he said. I could feel his eternal smile rippling along the lines. "I can't understand why," he went on. "I thought it was perfectly charming. One never knows."

"Do one," I said.

"But he told me he had offered you an assignment," Eric went on, "and I do hope you will accept that. It would be so good to have you on the team."

"Eric," I said, interrupting. "Something has come up." I hoped he wouldn't ask just what that was, since I wasn't quite sure myself. Was it my dander? My gorge? My lunch?

"An assignment, of course, would just be the beginning," Eric rattled on. "I'm sure you'll catch the hang of it in no time."

"Eric," I said, interrupting again. "We're going home."

As I hung up, nostalgia swept over me in waves. Home! How ready I was for that. How ready I was to stay there. I

102

had jumped the fences for a while, like a restless horse turned out to pasture. I had had my fling. I had tried Broadway, and I had tried Hollywood, and I had found each of them to be, whatever else they were, the refuge of unstable minds. A plague on both their houses.

I knew where I belonged. No matter what other considerations were involved, I belonged at my desk in my study at home, writing stories, as I had always done, and knew how to do, and found pleasure in the doing. We would have to come to terms with the other problems of our life from that premise.

CHAPTER SEVEN

Now that we were back home again our mornings began with little Billy Bailey. And what a blessing that was. If I were fortunate enough I might see him through the bathroom window as I shaved, while he came to us. He would have dressed himself, from what was apparently a wardrobe of such magnitude that almost never did he have to appear in the same outfit twice. Laura told us that his father said that Billy's room looked like an affluent slum. Billy, it seems, had aunts to burn, all of whom lavished gifts on him, and he wanted all of it out where he could see it all of the time.

It was my feeling that rather than an affluent slum, Billy's room, which I had never seen, must surely have looked more like a fitting room in the Brooks Costume Company, where actors went to be dressed for their roles. One day Billy might be a spaceman in a plastic helmet. The next day he could be an Indian, or a cowboy, or a private in the Army. The variations, and the props he carried were endless. But when Billy was a Marine Corps corporal he carried a gun which shot death-ray pellets, which were always turning up in odd corners of the house after he had gone, and were, in my opinion, not death-ray pellets at all, but those little arrows tipped with curare used by some South American Indians to paralyze their victims. We were powerless in the hands of Billy, Kate and I. He could do anything with us at all.

He was always up early, earlier, his father said, than the rest of them. He selected his own wardrobe and his character for the day from the disorder on the floor of his affluent slum. Once, when Kate had asked him what he was going to be when he grew up, he had said, "I'm going to be number one."

"Number one what?" Kate had asked, puzzled.

"I'm going to be the chief," Billy said, dancing away.

There was no reason whatever to doubt him. If ever there were a chief in the making, Billy Bailey was it. Of course he hadn't quite decided what he was going to be chief of. He was still trying out various roles.

When he had made his choice for the day, Billy couldn't wait to get outside. He would leap out from the kitchen door as if to a world which had been created for him fresh each day. He never walked. He ran, but his legs were still so short that often the steps became a kind of skip, so that he seemed to be dancing over the lawn. He missed nothing on the way, and as I watched him from my window I would be reminded that the history of the man is the history of the species. Billy Bailey was man. You felt that with him the race had been born anew, and that for him all of the discoveries and the wonder of man lay still ahead.

When he came to our house he would run around it in a circle before he came to the back door. I don't know why. He was big for his age, and his head was large even for that. But then, so were his ears and his mouth. They were like articles of clothing bought by some frugal mother several sizes too large, so that he might grow into them. He would grow into his ears and his head and his mouth, and, hopefully, even into his feet, which he sometimes tripped over as he ran, although he never admitted to this. "I was pretending to be a football player being tackled," he would say, as he fell all over himself. Again, the history of the man was the history of the species. Billy never admitted to error, and the truth was not in him. He made up his life as he went along, and then he justified it or explained it later, sometimes inserting chapters of fiction, just to give the whole thing more style.

For instance, no one could do more with one spoonful of jelly than Billy. Just as he was a man born to make his own bed and lie in it, so was he a man born to spread his own jelly. In the houses of most people the bread is usually rather well behaved, but in our house it was sometimes quite intractable. Often it insisted on flinging itself on the floor when it was half-spread, and it was expert at landing jelly side down. The thing to do then was to scale the kitchen sink with a great leap to capture a paper towel from the roll above, and then to wipe the floor, your hands, and the front of your shirt with it, so that the jelly might be evenly distributed over all surfaces.

"Is your mother going to be mad about that?" I said to Billy once, surveying his small person, which looked rather like one of those recently contemporary works of art where paint was thrown at the canvas instead of being applied with a brush.

Billy caressed his jersey, rubbing the jelly in. It hardly ever took him more than a second to make up an appropriate reply. "It's just my work shirt," he said.

But in the morning he was pristine. In fact he was so fresh, so new, so clean that it made your eyes ache just to look at him. When he had completed his circuit of the house, dancing and skipping, he would come to the kitchen door to ring the bell. It was not for me the bell tolled, and I learned early never to fool myself that it was. As every mother knows, little

106

boys and little girls are different from each other in every cell of their being from the moment they are born. Billy was a man-child, and it was Kate he came to see. He was her gentleman caller, but I didn't know that at first, thinking, in my simple-minded way, that he came to see both of us.

Kate and I did not have breakfast together. In a writer's house, where the husband is at home the whole, blessed, live-long day, certain methods of mutual protection are worked out. There is the story of the woman who said, with some despair, after her husband had retired, that she had married him for better or for worse, but not for lunch. Kate and I were married for better or for worse, but not for breakfast. Kate was hungry when she wakened and she liked to have breakfast at once, but I preferred to wait for that until after I had shaved.

This arrangement suited Billy ideally. When I came downstairs I would hear his pure little treble voice, chatting away to Kate. They would be sitting at the table in the dining room. Billy had possibly had his breakfast, or possibly he had not. In the interests of truth it was best not to ask. Meanwhile, he would consent to have a slice of toast with jelly, and a glass of orange juice, sitting in the master's chair at the head of the table. Together, they looked like a parody of a little old married couple. I would stop in the hall to listen. The sound of Billy's voice, like his presence in the house, seemed, as I have said, a sort of blessing, bestowed upon us at a time when all such blessings were in rather short supply. I never learned what it was they talked about, and after the first morning I never dared ask.

I had gone into the kitchen from the hall. It had been my intention to pour myself a cup of coffee and join them. Little Billy, erect at the heard of the table, was talking. When he heard me go into the kitchen from the hall, he got up from his chair, or down from it; he went to the door which led from the dining room into the kitchen, and closed it. He then apparently resumed his seat, and the interrupted monologue continued. I felt so rebuffed I had my cup of coffee in the kitchen behind the closed door.

There was a lot for the little couple to do in the mornings, after we had finished our respective breakfasts. My, but they were busy. I would have gone to my study, to the pleasure and the satisfaction of familiar work. In the kitchen the popsicle factory would be going into its morning shift. Kate had consulted with Laura about the decorum of the whole situation. "I love having Billy here," she said, "but I don't want to spoil him, and I certainly don't want to do anything for him, or give him anything that you wouldn't like."

With that, certain rules were laid down. They read something like the fasting rules for the Lenten season. One slice of toast after breakfast, a light collation in mid-morning, but never sweets before mealtimes, and soft drinks, with sugar in them, so bad for the teeth, were forbidden. So, out from their dusty storage, where they had hidden for so long that I had forgotten about them, came the popsicle molds. They were small triangular shells of aluminum. In the broad end was a small round hole encircled by a rubber washer, through which a dowell stick could be inserted. Into the molds with the stick inserted, natural fruit juice, unsweetened, was then poured, and the molds were carried, precariously, to the freezer.

This project soon became as complicated and as fraught with difficulties as the building of the Aswan Dam. There were never enough molds to meet the demand, since Suzy had to have her share when she appeared. Ideally, fresh molds would replace those that were removed, so that new popsicles would be in constant supply. When a popsicle was frozen it was removed from its mold by holding it for a moment under running water, until a push on the dowel stick would release it. The mold then had to be washed. Often the stick of the consumed popsicle was mislaid. New sticks had to be cut from the supply of dowels kept in the broom closet. There was a certain amount of attrition of materials in the process of manufacture. Sometimes it was impossible to cross the kitchen, since the heels of one's shoes became fixed in the fruit juice spilled on the floor.

Aside from all of this, Billy had to work on the maintenance of the special place which had been set aside for him in the refrigerator. This was where he kept his private fruit juice, and his personal jam. In the breadbox there was also a corner reserved for his favorite cookies. (On the shelf above the kitchen sink there was a place reserved for me, where I kept my personal water pistol, loaded and ready for self-defense.)

Between shifts, lemonade was prepared, not only for refreshment, but to be stored against the future in the refrigerator in the special place that belonged to Billy. For the purposes of the mid-morning light collation, at which toast was again served, the toaster had been permanently adjusted to achieve the degree of brownness preferred by Billy. And since the question of a choice of jelly was often insurmountable, the custom of two jellies had been introduced, and these two jellies were also stored in the reserved space in the refrigerator for Billy, which was, of course, off limits to other personnel.

With fruit juice on the floor, lemonade on the counter tops, jelly on every surface, and toast crumbs dusting all, soon the conquest was complete, and the whole kitchen had become Billy Bailey territory, over which the Billy Bailey ensign flew, bearing his personal heraldic device: two popsicles crossed on a field of lost sweaters.

It was into this conquered kingdom one morning that Betty Leonard came, our real-estate-agent neighbor, to whom Kate had written from Hollywood. In retrospect the entire Hollywood experience had come to seem a sort of delirium from which we had wakened again to reality, and not only had Kate and I forgotten the letter, it seemed impossible to imagine that it had ever been real, and had flown with an authentic stamp across the country. But it had, and Betty Leonard had taken it seriously, and now she had a prospective buyer for the house, a Mr. Stanton, a young businessman with a wife and small children, a family at that same stage of development we had been when we moved to the country. Would we be interested in selling to them?

It did not take us long to make up our minds about this. I had already made up my mind, definitely and without equivocation, out there in the used sunlight of Hollywood. I wanted to be where I was. And Kate followed along, with her own reasoning about that. She had enjoyed herself in California, but still, as she said, after a certain time in life it isn't possible to make intimate friends. You may make new frends in new and distant places, but they will never be to you as the friends of twenty years. In some way she had learned this, or had had this knowledge fortified, by going away and returning. We had always taken our friends and neighbors more or less for granted. We were, all of us in our village, rather like the separate cells of a corporate body which could at any given time coalesce and become one, in the face of a common threat such as, for example, a proposed super highway which would have cut us in two, or a possible change in zoning which might alter the residential character of our neighborhood, but for the most part we lived our private lives privately.

It was this unstated or unexamined attachment to our village which, once understood, provided us with our decision. We could leave the old house. We were permitted to do that. Our roots, our family roots were not there. The old house didn't need us any more. It needed the Stanton family, and the Stanton family needed it.

But we would never leave the village. We would keep a piece of our own land on which the old house stood, a wooded plot in the back, from which a lane could be cut through to the road. Here we would build a new house more suited to our present needs and our situation in life. Our roots would be undisturbed. We would still have our old friends and neighbors. We would still be neighbors of the Baileys.

On this innocent bit of earth which had never known, at least as far as we knew, any human conflict, our struggles began.

CHAPTER EIGHT

I HAD always assumed, with no evidence to the contrary, that if one wanted to build a house, and that if for this purpose one retained an architect and hired a contractor, they, in turn, built the house for you. This is not so. To build a house for one's self, or to have a house built for one's self is an experience so traumatic, on so many different levels of injury and assault, that one is never quite the same again. There is an old saying which runs to the effect that if you want something done well you must do it yourself. Everyone connected with the building of a house, from the architect to the laborer who pours the footings, has taken this proverb or maxim as a way of life, and since it is your house they are building, and since they assume that you will want it done well, they make quite certain that you will end up doing it all by yourself.

But I anticipate, for first I had to get a permit for the building of a house, and this meant that I must appear before a local board of my peers, men by nature more suspicious than I, and men certainly more virtuous than I. The public-spirited men who serve without recompense on civic boards do this by moonlighting from full-time jobs, and when they appear in the evening under the greenish glare of the globes in the hearing room of the township hall, they are usually so stupefied by a day's work topped by home cooking that it is difficult to feel that one is getting through to them, or, indeed, establishing any sort of two-way communication at all. There was an uneasiness, widespread in the township hall, from which I could seem to dissuade no one, that since I wanted to build a second house on property which I had once owned *in toto,* on which a house already stood, I might be of that dread breed, the "developer," disguised as a local country bumpkin, and that not merely a second house lurked in my scheming mind, but another ten or twenty, or even thirty. All I could think to do was to assume my best Uriah Heep manner, and stand before the tribunal humbly wringing my hands, while I was required to pledge fierce oaths. Would the proposed building create any traffic congestion? Would it result in any air pollution? Any nuclear fall out? Would it pose any moral threat to the community? I hesitated a minute over that one, but then I remembered, with relief, that Cam was safely married and had gone away. Promise them anything, I kept muttering to myself, but pay the fees. I had never before been afforded a glimpse into the interior workings of our local government, and now that I had it made me think, in some way, of those grisly stories one hears about surgeons who sew people up again after one hopeless look inside.

But at length the building permit arrived, and I nailed it up bravely, as instructed, to a tree at the end of our new-made lane. It was a square of cardboard with a red circle in the center, and on the tree it looked like a bull's eye for target practice, which in a certain way it was, for all at once the building materials began to zero in, the sand and the cinder blocks, and the lumber and the cement and the bricks. It was all very exciting. We could just glimpse the activity through the trees from the kitchen window, and it was impossible to stay away. "My only complaint," Kate would say, as we trudged back and forth, "is that it is just too far to walk to, and not quite far enough away to bother with the car."

I was unable to localize any complaint, for now a fearful sense of paralysis had come over me. For some reason that I cannot explain, it only dawned on me at that moment that if we built a new house we would have to get out of the old one, and it was when I surveyed that task that creeping lassitude came over me. How had Hercules felt, I wondered, when he was faced with the Augean stables? I knew that Hercules had a lot going for him, but what would he have done here?

Just a look at our stable was dismaying enough. In it the stalls, which had been built along the back, had been removed, and in their place was something Kate referred to as her potting shed. The potting shed was chaos surrounded by disorder, but it had its own little back door, so that you could slip in and out again at will without ever having to do anything about the mess. On the walls there were shelves filled with flower pots and garden tools, broken and whole. There were flats for seedlings piled against the wall, and on the floor there were wooden tubs holding various and mysterious mixtures of earth for particular purposes, unnamed, and all about were burlap bags and heavy paper bags filled with manure or lime or peat moss or vermiculite or what have you. Most of these bags had been chewed at by groundhogs or field mice, and when they were moved the contents spilled out on the floor.

In front of the area referred to as the potting shed, there were from the past, other voices, other rooms. Old automobile parts lay about like the bones of prehistoric monsters, and ranged on the shelves above was a carefully hoarded collection of peanut butter jars, which had been at one time lovingly filled with nuts and bolts and washers and screws and nails, even axle grease, and objects and sinister liquids, unknown to anyone but the original alchemist and master mechanic. They had all been placed there by the young master mechanic in happy, carefree days, filled with life in action. Now they moldered in silence, gathering dust, for the action had moved to another place, and their disposal would be the responsibility of those who were left behind.

There was also a loft in the barn which was used for storage, and in the way of friendly houses such as ours was, or as we had tried to make it, young people came and went, and the storage facility was extended to them. There was young Maggie who had gone to the Peace Corps, storing a part of her life with us before she left, in the attic of the house, as well as the loft of the barn. We thought she had taken it all away on her return from her two-year stint, but there was still a box of hers in the loft with textbooks in it, and now Maggie was off somewhere in Latin America. One of the textbooks was Gray's *Anatomy,* which might come in very handy some day, when we tried to put ourselves together in the new house. There was also a portable bar up there in the loft, covered with fake leather, which dated from the bachelor-apartment days of the young master mechanic and one of his raffish friends. Now that they had both been trapped into matrimony, its existence was probably forgotten by them, as well as that of the sofa with the sagging springs which they had carried up there at the same time, as if preserving for some ungrateful posterity the artifacts of a period of hedonistic pursuit better left buried. There were also pasteboard boxes up there, tied with cord, stacks of them, on which paper labels were pasted, listing the contents, but the ink on the labels had faded, and no one remembered what was inside.

Inside the house it was even worse, if such a thing could be imagined. The cellar under the kitchen, for example, was the oldest part of the house, with thick stone foundation walls dating from the early eighteenth century, and at one memorable moment in the history of the house an effort had been made to turn this cellar into a bomb shelter, since it could be entered from outside down steps to its own door, beneath a sloping roof, which corresponded almost exactly in design to the plan for a bomb shelter which was handed out at our county seat.

The work on the bomb shelter had been a sort of distraction, a counter-irritant, like hitting yourself on the head with a hammer to forget the pain of a broken toe. It was when Cam had been doing his stint in the Coast Guard, and suddenly we were in the midst of the Cuban crisis, with the Soviet shipment of arms on its way.

I don't think we cared so much about ourselves. I think we rather felt like a neighbor friend, a gallant woman living alone who said she couldn't be bothered with a bomb shelter even if the courthouse did want us all to have one. "If a bomb falls," she said, "I'm just going to run outside and go with the crowd."

I think we would have wanted to go with the crowd too, if the time came, but there was Cam, and he was not just our son, he was the future of our race, and if war came even the Coast Guard would be involved, so there was a mother in our house who couldn't sleep at night, and who got up to do things to keep herself busy: nice, sensible, rational things like processing drinking water in Mason jars in the pressure cooker, to carry down to shelves in the old cellar.

I helped her make a project of it when I found out what

she was doing. It kept both of us occupied and distracted. We checked the list of recommended items for storage in a bomb shelter which was distributed at the courthouse. We made trips in the afternoons back and forth to various stores. We bought tins of beans and beef stew and corned beef hash. We brought home candles and matches, and tins to put them in. We bought cots at the Army and Navy store, and battery-powered flashlights and a battery-powered radio, and even a portable latrine.

Most of that stuff was all still down there in the cellar, forgotten, since, happily for our natures, nothing is forgotten more quickly than anxiety, once the threat is removed. But there were even more things down there, in the larger cellar beyond the old cellar. Things such as cans of paint, half filled, and carpentry tools, and boxes of old fuses, and a clutter of broken objects meant to be repaired, sagging with dust and neglect. Even Hercules would have been daunted.

And then there was the attic. I have heard it said by a competent physiologist that no one actually knows very much about the human brain, and possibly very little of it is used in our daily lives. I imagine that the attic of any old house such as ours might be described in the same way. Certainly no one knew very much about what was up there, and very little of it was used in our daily lives.

To get to the attic you had to pull down a little set of folding steps which you let down from the ceiling in the upstairs hall, and if you inched your way up this precarious foothold and stuck your head over the top you were confronted by a welter of picture frames, old furniture, boxes and trunks, and storage bags for clothes hanging from hooks. In the trunks there were things from the houses of different grandmothers, which had come to us in a way I no longer remembered. Over the years there had been vague talk about giving the clothing in the trunks to some museum or other, but I had an awful feeling that other people had got to the museums first with their grandmothers' trunks, and that we might be too late, even with the parasols that were tied up in one corner.

There were more recent clothes up there too, such as wedding dresses. Wedding dresses seem much more hallowed than wedding suits, for what reason I do not know, although it may mean that most men tend to put the past behind them more completely than women do, as witness the forgotten bachelor bar and sagging sofa in the loft in the barn. My own wedding suit was at one time cut into strips to become part of a rag rug. Although I said nothing about it at the time, my feelings were rather hurt. But I have since concluded that it was a commendable solution to the problem, and I wonder if the same thing might be done with me when the time comes.

Writers, unlike many men, do not put the past behind them so quickly. A writer's raw material is the past and he is prone never to throw anything away. In files in the attic there was every letter I had ever received, along with copies of a good many I had sent out. It was my hostage to life. Sometimes I mined those files, as a prospector might go looking for gold. Also in the attic was everything I had ever written, published or unpublished, in its original form, and while this was a considerable quantity, it did not pose quite the same difficulty as the accumulated letters, for manuscripts, unlike unwieldy filing cases, come in tidy stacks and may be carried easily from one storage place to another.

I thought perhaps I should do something about those letters. Perhaps I could consolidate, thin out, discard. I might make them less of a burden to carry to the new house. In its way, this decision was a mistake.

I carried the letter files down the attic stairs and put them into an empty guest room. For about a week I sat there every afternoon in a comfortable chair, under a reading lamp, to go through them, in sequence, as I had never done when going to them idly for corroboration, or for material. When or if we think about our lives at all, I suppose we think in retrospect that they have some sort of continuity. One event leads to another, and we go on, generally too busy to remember what went before.

It is not easy to review twenty years of one's life. If you are foolhardy enough to attempt this you will find that the sense of continuity you felt existed is, in fact, an illusion. Life is a process of false starts and hopes unfulfilled, of failure and loss, along with whatever happiness we are able to garner along the way. We remember the happiness, but we forget the pain.

I went through those letters of twenty years. I did not throw very much away. Life, as one writer said, is an unhappy story. The hero always dies in the end. But one does not like to be reminded of this too often, and meanwhile I would just go on adding to the files, as the living coral builds on the reef below.

When I had abandoned this task, I walked over through the field and the trees to see how the new house was going, as I did at the end of every day after the workmen had gone. There were moments when we were summoned to the site during the day while the workmen were still there, for some decision or other, and these command appearances were to become more frequent, but as yet the new house had not demanded all of our time.

The scent of fall was in the air. I felt a sense of foreboding as the season advanced. The contractor promised us that we would be in the house before winter came, but so much remained to be done that I began to feel apprehensive about

119

this. The foundation was in, the framework of the house had gone up. The roof had been laid on. On the day the rooftree had been set in place, the architect had come to us to say that a celebration was in order. One of the older workmen with a sense of tradition had cut a young sapling and carried it up the ladder to nail to the ridgepole, or rooftree. We carried glasses out to the lawn, and a bottle of wine, and under the trees we drank a toast with the workmen to the new house.

It had been a happy moment. I had wondered if it was then that the animus of the house had entered it. Every house has its soul, a spiritual being quite apart from those who happen to live in it. Certainly I had come to know the animus of the old house well, when I sat up with it at night, having my nightcap, as with an old friend.

But now as I stood in the gray twilight with the suspicion of an autumnal chill in the air, and looked at the frame skeleton of the house, at the new brick of the chimney, at the piles of building material scattered about, I wondered how this house could ever come alive. And if and when it did, would it be a happy house? That sense of apprehension came over me. If change was indicated, was this change in our lives the best for us? Was the time ill advised? Was it all a mistake?

CHAPTER NINE

MEANWHILE, back at the house, things were also going not at all well for Kate. She was having her own problems with the confrontation of the past and the future, but they were practical problems which could not be resolved in the mind at some distant time, but had to be settled now. Of the possessions we had, which would fit into the new house and which would not? Kate had a floor plan of the house as it would be when finished, supplied to her by the architect, with the measurements of the dimensions of the rooms in all directions, and this, together with an old straw knitting bag, which was filled with samples of carpeting, curtain and drapery material, wallpaper, slipcover and upholstery fabric, was her constant companion; she could be seen at almost any moment, wandering about like some poor mad Ophelia, brushing bits of straw from her hair, and if I were not very careful I would find myself involved in much the same sort of scene which had once confounded Hamlet. "There is too much orange in the green," she would croon, holding bits of paper or cloth to the walls, or moving, dreamlike, to the window, to expose

121

them to light. "It will not go with the blue of the rug, because there is too much pink in the blue."

I was alarmed for her. Mr. Bowman, our contractor, was also concerned about her. There was some pathetic, deranged creature further back in the county, for whom Mr. Bowman was also building a new house, and her husband had just taken her to the hospital, although Mr. Bowman couldn't swear to it that it was a mental hospital.

"She changed the color of the paint for the living room walls three times," Mr. Bowman said, "and then just as the painter started to paint with the color she had finally decided on, she went into hysterics. That's when her husband took her away."

No matter how many years he has been married, any man will tell you that he learns new things about his wife almost every day. Building a house with Kate not only opened up to me whole new vistas of her personality, but also threatened to unhinge me, although the salesman in a place called the decorating center, which gradually became something like a second home to us, told me not to worry. I will never again be able to look without emotion at a doorknob, or a kitchen cabinet, or the tile in a bathroom shower in any house we visit, for I now know that these things did not just appear there. They had to be selected, and to select them the buyer is forced to go to them, for the manufacturers of these objects hoard them in showrooms, and part with them only with the utmost reluctance, after a waiting period cunningly designed to drive the most hardy into the nearest straitjacket.

But as the days passed, and the days became weeks, as we were drawn deeper and deeper into the vortex, the salesman at the decorating center urged me to be reassured about myself. Only women, he insisted, really lost their minds while building a house.

"I have a customer now, she's on the verge," he said. "Yesterday, ten minutes before they were to lay the tiles in her kitchen, she came in here, all wild-like, sobbing, you know, to say that they had to be changed because they didn't go with the formica on the top of the cabinets. And the workmen were in the house!"

"May I ask a question?" Kate called from the other end of the showroom. "Is it too late to change the tiles in the bathroom?"

Clearly, something had to be done. I had to take Kate away for a few days, even for a weekend, and even if I had to carry her from the scene, before the men in the white coats came to get her.

But when I broached this idea she was adamant. How could she entertain the thought of leaving, even for a day, when there was nothing but incompetence and disorder and confusion on all sides? How could we leave when decisions were required of us every day? Had she not rescued us from disaster when she had discovered, for example, that the light globes on the screened porch had been installed flush with the ceiling, instead of being suspended on stems, as ordered? Could we have lived with such ugliness the rest of our lives? Had she not discovered in the garden court—which was never, under any circumstances, to be called a patio—that the bricks were being put down in the wrong pattern? And what if the kitchen cabinets should come while we were away? Could she trust anyone to put them up correctly in her absence? Maybe there were people so irresponsible, so flighty, she said, looking pointedly in my general direction, that *they* could pick up and leave while a house was being built for them, by a unique assemblage of workmen who were all thumbs and left hands; but *someone* had to be responsible, *someone* had to stay on the scene to see that things were done right, *some-one* . . .

"Someone may end up in the booby hatch," I said, "and I don't think they very much care there whether the light bulbs come on stems or not."

Kate was silent. Impotent silence. She was surrounded by nincompoops. What could be done? What could she do?

"Try to think back," I said. "Where were you happiest in your whole life? Before you got mixed up with me and a new house and unsatisfactory things like that. Where were you the most carefree? Where did you feel absolutely relieved of all responsibility?"

Well, it certainly didn't take very long to remember that. That was the Hotel Buckingham. That was Atlantic City. That was with Grandmother, when she was a little girl. But she couldn't go back there now. She couldn't leave.

Still, the idea had been planted in her mind. She slept on it. Or rather she did not sleep on it, since sleep was rather hard to come by these days, what with so many responsibilities on her shoulders. She got up with wakened memories of Atlantic City, and at luncheon time she mused about them. In retrospect it seemed a sort of Nirvana or Shangri-La. They had always gone to Atlantic City in the summer when she was a child. They had always stayed at the Hotel Buckingham. In those halcyon days there was never any confusion or disorder. Serenity was the order of the day. Everyone was kind, and everyone was loving. Everyone was also competent. It was difficult when you thought about it, to understand how this dreadful thing had taken place. The Garden of Eden was a long way back, but by what steps had she come so far from it? Here she was now, surrounded by delay and obstruction, by contractors who didn't contract, by architects who disappeared, by carpenters and electricians and plumbers who were obviously imposters in masquerade.

"I think I could put up with a lot of it," Kate said, "if I just had my outlets."

To an outsider this might have seemed a reasonable alternative, suggesting visions of basket-weaving or finger painting, but this was not exactly what Kate referred to. In working in the kitchen of the new house, the left-handed carpenters had unaccountably covered the electrical wiring in such a way that the cables for the electrical outlets could not be found. Kate had planned a bank of such outlets, a splendor of modern convenience, so that all of her equipment, the toaster, the mixing machine, the blender might all be there at once, ready for instant use. Now they had left her with only one outlet, which was all that she had had in the past. It was hardly worth the effort of moving. The new stove had been installed. It listed, and the exhaust fan in the hood above was defective, and who knew what to do about that? The new faucet in the new kitchen sink had come off in her hand when she had turned it on to test it. The material for the curtains for our new bedroom had been lost in shipment and would have to be traced. That morning she had been unable to find the proper mate for her shoe, which possibly wasn't too important since all of her shoes were so covered with mud from going back and forth to the new house that no one could have told left from right anyway. There was a leak in the new roof, and a thin stream of water ran down the wall in the front hall when it rained, which was most of the time. Outside the leaves were turning gold. Inside our hair was turning gray.

"Did you telephone Mr. Bowman?" Kate asked. It was a routine question, so mechanical that it might have saved time and effort to have it taped, so that it could have been played at the customary intervals of about fifteen minutes apart.

"I did," I said. "Mr. Bowman has had a tooth extracted. He is at home in bed and his wife is giving him brandy."

"Isn't there anything you can do?" Kate asked.

"I could go out and get some brandy for us," I said.

"I could go out of my mind," Kate said.

"That's just what I have been talking about," I said. "Don't you think Atlantic City is a much more reasonable solution?"

Kate got up to clear the table. "Maybe they wouldn't have room for us at the Hotel Buckingham," she said, her back to me.

I leaped for the telephone. It was a Thursday. If we left in the morning, on Friday, we could have a long weekend away. The information operator found the Hotel Buckingham for me. It was really there, not just a dream. And they did have a room for us.

In the morning as we were getting ready to leave, Billy appeared as usual. He was wearing a new Batman cape and mask. In the building of the new house, Billy had been the most dependable of all the men on duty. From the moment the bulldozer had arrived, Billy had taken charge. Every time I looked out of my window I could see him. He was in the foundation. He was on it. He was outside of it. He was standing on the pile of building blocks. He was leaping from pile to pile of earth. It was his self-appointed duty, apparently, to entertain the men while they were at work so they wouldn't finish too soon. He was the mascot of the project. The men loved him. Mr. Bowman, a producer of daughters, threatened to kidnap him and take him home.

This morning he needed a handkerchief before he could go on duty. He wheezed as he spoke, since Batman's nose wasn't quite where his nose was. Kate brought him a handkerchief, and thinking I could trick him out of the mask,

which looked and sounded so uncomfortable, I said, "Whatever happened to Billy Bailey, Batman? Have you seen him
around?"

"They shot him," Billy said, blowing his nose.

There was the sound of a car in the driveway. It was the
unexpected arrival of Mr. Bowman. Billy ran out to greet
him, and I followed behind.

Mr. Bowman was a short, stout, ruddy man who used words
sparingly, on the principle, I think, that if you give too much
candy to a child it may spoil him. Mr. Bowman's face was
swollen on one side and he had a sort of brandy look about
the eyes. Mr. Bowman was always cheerful, even in disaster,
but I think that may have been because he had never known
anything but disaster in his life. He was sorry about the delay,
he said, and he had come to check the leak in the new roof.
Unfortunately, no one else would be present today. The elec-
trician had gone away for a few days on his doctor's orders
because of his nerves. The plumber had been bitten by a toy
poodle. The carpenter had hit his thumb with a hammer. We
had already learned how fragile most building men were, in
spite of their deceptively rugged appearance, and now our
sick list was complete.

"How is your jaw?" I asked Mr. Bowman.

"The doctor gave me an injection," he said.

I was tempted to ask him if he had gone off the brandy, but
I hesitated. It remained to be seen if Mr. Bowman functioned
better on the needle than on the bottle.

"We are going to Atlantic City for a few days," I said to
Mr. Bowman. "We will be back on Monday." Kate had not
come out. She stood behind us in the doorway. She had
formed a conviction that building contractors didn't like
women, and she kept her distance. Perhaps they didn't. There
are always two sides to every question.

127

"May I ask you a question?" Kate called. "Do you think you will ever be able to find my outlets?"

Mr. Bowman pretended not to hear. "There is a list of things that still remain incompleted," I said, handing him a sheet of paper Kate had prepared for him. Kate could not have heard us, but I found myself speaking in a sort of conspiratorial whisper. "Please see if you can't get at least a few of these things done while we are away," I said. "I would hate to come back to the same old problems."

Mr. Bowman took the list, shaking his head. He put his hand to his jaw in silence. It was no time to spoil me with a word of comfort. He turned and went off toward the new house, guarded on all sides by Batman.

And then we were off, with our bags in the car, heading toward the Garden State Parkway, trailing tangled threads of disorder and frustration behind us.

"I don't think the roof on the courtyard should be of that plastic stuff," Kate said, "no matter how new and interesting it is supposed to be. I think it is going to look cheap. I asked Mr. Bowman if I could see a part of it in place before it was all up, but he didn't answer me. Of course I know Mr. Bowman doesn't like women."

A car went by us very fast and I swerved to avoid it, also resolving to avoid any discussion of plastic versus glass, along with other particularly controversial subjects, all of which had been gone over at least two dozen times.

Kate fastened her seat belt. "When we get back I'm going to call Mrs. Perkins," she said. "Maybe she will know what to do about the welting on the slipcovers. If we used blue it would tie in with the rug, but of course it would have to be a warm blue. A cold blue would kill everything."

"Do you think it might work on the crab grass?" I asked.

"I hope you gave the list to Mr. Bowman," Kate said.

"I did," I said.

"Not that it will make any difference," Kate said. "We're never going to be finished. I just know that. Nothing is ever going to come out right."

"We'll have to have patience," I said. "Everything is bound to seem out of kilter for a while, even after we get into the new house. I've been thinking that it will be sort of like a shakedown cruise. You know, I was on one in the Navy. When they build a new ship they send it out on a trial cruise, just to get all the bugs out."

"Yes, I know," Kate said. "You've told me all about that. Several times. Was there a captain in charge?"

I ignored that remark. We sped over the Jersey marshes for a while in silence.

"Do you really like the color for the bedroom walls?" Kate said. "I do wish you would really tell me while there is still time to change."

"I love it," I said, trying to remember just what color the walls of the bedroom were going to be. "I wouldn't have it any other way."

"But you say that about all the colors!" Kate said. She took a pocket handkerchief from her handbag and held it to her eyes. There are places in the tropics, I am told, where it rains on schedule for half an hour every morning, and this natural phenomenon had begun to take place at our house.

"It's all so hopeless!" Kate said, her words muffled by her handkerchief. "I wish we had never done it! Sometimes I think it was all a terrible mistake! Oh, I wish we had never sold the house!"

There was no answer to that. The house was sold, irrevocably. We had to be out of it in less than two months.

"When we get to the next exit let's stop for lunch," I said.

"I want to hear all about the Hotel Buckingham again before we get to it."

Over a chicken salad and a cup of tea, Kate was persuaded to take up her reminiscences again about that lost Eden. They had gone to Atlantic City first when she was about five, she thought, and they had gone every summer after that. They went by train, and at the station at Atlantic City a carryall would be waiting for them, with the name of the Hotel Buckingham emblazoned on its sides. The carryall opened at the back, and inside there were seats upholstered in black leather. Wonderful, smiling colored men in white coats were there to lift them from the train, to swing them up into the carryall. They rode off to the Hotel Buckingham, and settled with all of their trunks into endless rooms, and lived happily ever after.

"What did you do with yourself all day?" I asked.

A rapt look came over Kate's face. "We dug holes in the sand," she said, dreamily. "When it rained we played inside in the children's playroom, and we had our dinner in the children's dining room. With our nursemaid, of course."

Of course. Nursemaids, and smiling retainers, and now here she was on a leaky ship without a captain.

"Father came on weekends," Kate said, "and sometimes even Grandfather came, and how they spoiled us! They bought us anything we asked for, and Gordon and I used to run up and down the Boardwalk with those toys you pull with a string, ducks that flapped their wings, and dogs on wheels. We laughed all the time," she said, beginning to cry again.

"I wish you could give me a sample of how that went," I said.

"Did you ever see the horse jump off the end of the Steel Pier?" Kate asked, smiling at me bravely, moistly, over the top of her handkerchief.

"No," I said. "But I think I can understand how he felt."

"Oh, I have so many things to show you!" Kate said.

"Well, let's go," I said, reaching for the check.

And so we came to the Hotel Buckingham.

It lay under a magic spell. From afar it could be seen, as you sped over the causeway toward the sea, rising in the distance like Camelot. Its towers and cupolas and turrets stood against the sky like a Walt Disney fairy-tale castle, and as you approached it more closely you could see that nothing but the best marzipan had gone into its construction. Festoons and garlands of marzipan flowers and fruits hung from its balconies and encircled its towers; urns of rock candy blossomed with spun-sugar flowers, and great arches of caramel blocks led to its doors, where elves in livery waited to carry the bags.

Inside all was Aubrey Beardsley. In the great lobby tree trunks of white fondant climbed against white fondant walls, reaching upward with curlicue branches of white fondant to blossoms which held unshaded light bulbs. Acres of carpeted space were filled with acres of sofas and writing desks, but as we looked around our hearts sank, for inside the Hotel Buckingham, something had gone terribly wrong with the magic spell. Everything was just as it had been. Nothing had changed. Time had stood still. Except for the people. Everyone, including the help, had grown old in this geriatric paradise.

We went up to our room, preceded by the aging pixie who carried our bags. It was a pretty room. There was a bay window which looked down upon the spun-sugar flowers, and the windows stood slightly open so that the curtains stirred in the sea breeze. It was furnished as every room had been furnished in all the summer hotels in which one had stayed as a child. There were two brass beds. There was a desk in the bay window with a cane-seated chair pulled up to it, and there was a rocking chair, and a wicker armchair. There was comfort everywhere, even if you knew that the walls had been painted a thousand times.

Kate curled up on one bed. "Well, I guess we came here to rest," she said, in a child's voice. She turned her face to the wall, and I pulled a summer blanket over her.

In an hour we were out on the Boardwalk. It was a beautiful fall day, a day of Indian summer, when summer, apparently remorseful about its past excesses, comes back to soothe you with bright skies and cool air. The ocean lay becalmed beside us, as unruffled as a lake. Breakers crested far out, catching the light, and rolled majestically to stretches of white sand. Hand in hand we walked along the endless bleached boards which stretched before us like eternity.

I don't think it was passion that made us hold hands. When you have been married as long as Kate and I have been married you learn that something takes the place of passion. I suppose there might be disbelief among some if I were to say that what takes the place of passion is almost better than passion, but that can't be explained, because you won't know about it until you get there. Anyway, we also held hands to help maintain our equilibrium. On the endless boardwalk at Atlantic City, which stretches at such dizzying length in front of one, there is no place to sit down, except for a few enclosures with benches which seem to contain lifetime inhabitants, some of them as young as seventy. The unspoken suggestion is that you hire a rolling chair, but after an hour or so of this you learn that it is cheaper to risk exhaustion. On either side of us as we walked were the mixed blandishments of this ancient pleasure dome, the auction galleries, the hot dog stands, the salt-water taffy emporiums, women's shops, men's shops, shooting galleries, and peanut galleries.

"I have a little headache," Kate said. "A sort of nagging pain at the back of my head. Do you have any aspirin in your pocket?"

"No," I said. "But there is a drug store just ahead. I can see the sign."

We were not to make it that far, for just at that moment we came abreast of a jewelry auction gallery, and in the window was a sign announcing that inside was the recently acquired jewel collection of one of the late great beauties of the world, whose passing had been reported at some length in the newspapers. It drew Kate like a magnet. Her feet turned as if guided by radar, and holding hands we went in. At least it was a place to sit down. At least it was free. As long as you weren't tempted to buy anything, a temptation which didn't exist for us, not, at least, while we were building a house.

"We're building a house," Kate said to the salesman, over the trays of jewels he brought to her, reverentially, as if he were making an offering at the shrine of a goddess. "When you're building a house," Kate said, "you can't afford to buy anything else."

"Look anyway," the salesman said, smiling his enameled smile, the light striking from his oiled hair as well as from the diamonds. "It won't cost you a cent," he said. "Be my guest. Maybe you'll think it over and come back."

Kate was seduced. She hung necklaces worth a gangster's ransom around her neck. She slipped rings on her fingers, bracelets on her wrists. Her eyes shone. She was utterly absorbed, utterly lost to everything else. It pleased me to see her so happy, if only for a moment. Sometimes in life we succeed in maneuvering ourselves into a blind alley, so that we feel we can't go forward and we can't go back. I knew Kate felt

133

that way about the house. Her retreat was cut off, and she couldn't see any clear way ahead.

It was with a sigh that she finally relinquished the jewelry. She stood up. We thanked the salesman, and made our way out again to the boardwalk.

"There's the drug store just ahead," I said. "We can stop there for the aspirin."

"Oh, I don't have a headache now," Kate said. "It's gone."

"Great," I said. "When did it leave you?"

For a moment there was a flash of the old Kate in her eyes. "I believe it left me," she said, "while I was looking at the emeralds."

We laughed and went on, holding hands. There was nothing to do now but face up to it, and go back to the hotel for dinner.

The dining room at the Hotel Buckingham was an endless sea of gray-haired ladies. They came on canes and in wheelchairs, with their nursemaids or without, and the aged retainers who served them at the tables looked scarcely sturdy enough to lift the trays. Going through the corridors to the dining room, Kate had looked into reading rooms and the rooms for writing. She had opened doors, and rounded corners hopefully, as if some part of that golden past might still lie in wait for her, but there were television sets now in what had been the children's playroom, and if there was a children's dining room we could not find it.

But the ladies were cheerful. Many of them were still beautiful, and it was obvious that all of them took great care with their dress. Because it seemed necessary to maintain some sort of conversation after we had been seated at a table and ordered a cocktail, I looked out over the acres of marcelled heads, and picked a topic. It went like this:

"What is this obsession women have about their hair?" I

said. Even in making small talk I knew there was nothing like going to the horse's mouth for information, and even with age differences aside, there wasn't a single woman in that whole dining room who was any more obsessed with her hair than Kate Wallace.

"Women like their hair to be neat," Kate said, absently. The cocktails had come, and Kate took a sip from hers. She looked sadly around the room, and then she looked away.

"Neat!" I said. "A man likes his hair to be neat too, and it takes about thirty seconds."

"You don't understand," Kate said. "If a woman feels her hair isn't right, then it doesn't matter if she is wearing a dress by Givenchy. She won't feel right."

"Then women don't fix their hair for men?" I said, looking about the room at our neighbors who surely must have given up any thought of amorous conquest a long time ago.

"In a way they do," Kate said, listlessly.

"Doesn't it ever occur to a woman to just brush her hair?" I said, pushing on. "Or just to run a comb through it? Why do they have to spend so much time on it?"

"But that's exactly what I tell my hairdresser every week," Kate said, righteously. "I always tell her to do it so that it won't take any care."

Whenever Kate spoke with her Alice-in-Wonderland logic I knew that we were not communicating. On several levels, at the moment. Still, there was this puzzling thing about women and their hair. The mystique of the woman's crowning glory. I would never understand it, but I talked on, because the Hotel Buckingham was full of ghosts, and they had to be kept beyond the circle of the candlelight.

"Do men do anything that seems to women as persistently nutty?" I asked. "I mean as nutty as all this nonsense about hair?"

Kate looked thoughtful for a moment. "I wouldn't know

where to begin," she said. "But, well, it does give you a sort of a lift to go to a hairdresser. What do men do when they want a lift?"

"Sometimes they go to a bar," I said.

"There you are," Kate said with finality, as if the subject were closed.

"You mean it's like being an alcoholic?" I said. "You mean women are as hung up on their hair as a lush is on the sauce?"

Kate didn't answer. She didn't want to play the game any more. Dinner had arrived. She picked up her fork and looked at me. The threat of a tropical storm was there again in her eyes. "I suppose you can't go home again," she said. "They always say that. But I don't want to stay here. In the morning let's go back—to whatever it is we have."

In the morning we packed our bags and went down to the car. The doorman and the porter helped us assemble ourselves. "Come back!" they said, standing there in their Walt-Disney, Prince-Rupert-of-Hentzau uniforms. "There is still a lot of good weather ahead! Come back! Come back!"

We thanked them and drove away, back over the causeway, back to the Garden State Parkway. Back to whatever it was we had done with our lives. The weather still held. Indian summer enfolded us. The leaves of the trees were scarlet and gold, and the autumn air was still as we drove on, and pulled at last into the new lane which led to the new house, to see that first before going back to the old house.

There were no workmen there, but there it sat in its sea of dried mud, with the planks put down over bricks to get to the front door. But something had happened to it in our absence. It had somehow, unaccountably, pulled itself together. The light from the sun struck in through the uncurtained windows, and there was a kind of immobility about it, the immobility of equilibrium, as if all the stone and brick and timber and lath and plaster had suddenly discovered itself to be a house.

Kate ran quickly along the planks and threw open the front door. I followed her inside and watched her as she went about, touching things with a kind of wonder, as if she were Madame Ranevsky in *The Cherry Orchard* in reverse, not saying farewell to the past, but greeting a future.

"It's our house!" she said suddenly, turning to me. "It isn't anyone else's house! It's our house! It's the house we built! Oh, I really couldn't see that before," she said, moving about, opening doors, looking out of windows, running her hands along the walls. "I couldn't see the forest because of the trees."

She came to me. "Isn't it beautiful?" she said. "Think how dreadful it would be to have to stay forever and grow old in the Hotel Buckingham? Or even in our old house?"

She put her arms around me, under my arms, and I held her, thinking how difficult it is sometimes to escape from the past, how hard it is to break old patterns. And even when you wanted to do that, it wasn't always easy to find the right road. We had had to go down a couple of dead-end streets before we found the way ahead for ourselves.

"We have a whole new life ahead of us," Kate said, leaning her head against my shoulder.

"A whole new life," I said, hearing in my own voice the same sense of awe that was in hers.

"And I have you," Kate said, beginning to laugh a little. "Although I do wonder sometimes why you put up with me."

"Some people are just born lucky," I said.

In the empty room, with its smell of all things new, we stood and held each other, tightly, and at that moment the animus of our new house entered, silently, and took up residence there.

CHAPTER TEN

As I understand it, in my sketchy knowledge of history, civilization is supposed to have begun when men learned to plant grain, and to settle long enough in one place to harvest it, thus ending the nomadic wanderings of our ancestors. This is easy enough to believe, since it is always a man we see behind the plow, but at what point in time did women begin to plant flowers? Could it be that what went before was merely survival, and that civilization really began at that moment?

In the city of Madrid in Spain you may see the fountain of Cybele, an elaborate display of waterworks presided over by the ample figure of that goddess of the forces of nature, in a chariot drawn by horses. Aside from the fact that Cybele is more formidable, and more rounded, Kate could have, at any moment, taken her place, for if not fountains at least flowers sprang up in her wake, and all living things came into being about her as if by magic.

But one must not be deceived. It was not magic. There was a great deal of work involved, which began with the precious catalogues from White Flower Farm, and Wayside Gardens, and Mr. Burpee. Trees, plants, seeds arrived by express, by air, by mail, while great bundles of manure and mulch and lime were carted in, and often the sounds of discord were in the air, as the goddess drove on the local and temporary help she had managed to recruit to help her in the landscaping of the new house, after the winter had passed and spring had come.

I wish now I had a series of time-lapse photographs to show the miracle of change whereby the desert bloomed, and the film of green grass crept swiftly over the wasteland, while pachysandra rooted itself at foundations and at the bases of trees. Dogwood bloomed where no dogwood had bloomed before; lilacs opened their opulent, sensuous blossoms, like details in an ornamental Renaissance frieze. Fruit trees flowered, tubs appeared with fragrant oleander, and I began to know how that first primitive ancestor of mine had felt when he planted the corn, and waited for it to ripen. He may have fed his goddess, or provided the food by which she was fed, but it was she who brought the tulips in, to put in bowls, and the freesia, and the sweet-smelling roses.

"But it is curious," Kate often said, brushing a stray lock of hair back from her face with an earth-stained hand. "I'm so very happy, and yet I'm so depressed. I love it all here so much, I wish I didn't have to think."

For now that we were settled in our new house we discovered how self-directed our thoughts had been in the recent past, how inward we had become in our efforts to uproot ourselves and plant ourselves again, oblivious to how threatened the world around us was by the winds of social change.

"If only things would stand still long enough for us just to catch our breath," Kate said.

But of course nothing does stand still. You can try to make it stand still, or you may try to ignore it, if you are able to do this. Kate's way to try to ignore it was to work in her garden.

The world was too much with us. It was there behind the new hedge of hawthorn in the Bailey house, where we now learned at last that not Billy and Suzy and Laura alone lived, but also father Tim. That man of whom we had seen little but a casual wave of the hand when he came home from his office in the evening, now loomed large in our life, as a symbol, perhaps, of that new predicament in which we found ourselves, of exhilaration mingled with depression, of private happiness versus a concern for the world. We were not to be permitted to ignore the problems of our world, and who would have known that it would be Tim Bailey of the casual wave who would bring them to our door.

"People go through three phases with me," Tim said. "At least those people do who are my friends." We were sitting in the library of our new house. It was the end of what was for us a typical day of that first spring, that first beautiful spring of our new house and our new life. I had finished my work and closed up shop for the day, which for me was symbolized by putting the dust cover on my typewriter. I had lighted a fire in the fireplace. It was not really cool enough to justify a fire, but it seemed so pleasant to have the flames inside, and the green grass beyond the long windows, with daffodils in the woods beyond, and the fiddlehead ferns showing through the carpet of leaves. Kate had made a beautiful room for us, with the walls lined with books, and a comfortable sofa and chairs, and an old mahogany card table at which we often sat to have our dinner when we were alone.

Kate was in the kitchen, and I hoped she would stay there. Kate's routine at the end of her day was to wash the earth from her hands, take off her gardening clothes, and soak herself in the tub, happily reviewing all that she had planted or tended that day. After the tub she would brush her hair until it shone, and then she would put on something feminine, a long gown of some sort, of flowered silk or cotton. She would scent herself with something I liked, and then she would go into the kitchen to finish up the dinner preparations she had begun earlier in the day.

As I said, I hoped she would stay there for a while. We had suddenly a beautiful life, and perhaps it was selfish of us to think that we had earned it, but we were frankly selfish about wanting to protect it, and now here was Tim Bailey, possibly not meaning to, but doing his best to upset the applecart. If Kate were to come in to sit with us I would see her choler rise. My dictionary says that choler, used as a word to describe irritation or anger, is an archaic form, but the men who wrote my dictionary didn't know Kate. So I listened as she happily banged her pots and kettles, and hoped she would stay there.

"People at first usually like me," Tim said. Tim was holding a glass of beer. I was drinking something a little stronger, which I had at first offered Tim, but he said that as a family man he couldn't afford to cultivate more expensive tastes, and so he stuck to beer. We learned to have a few cans for him in the refrigerator. And as he spoke I looked at him and I knew that vanity did not prompt his words. People would like Tim Bailey at first sight. He was a likeable young man. He was physically all of a piece. He had a neatly made head, and tidy ears. His hair had once been fair, I suppose, but it had darkened. He had very blue eyes. There was a warm tone about him, a feeling of physical warmth. He smiled easily, and to first look at him you wouldn't know how far out he was. Indeed he was so far out that there was no reason to want to reach him except to punch him in the mouth. To look at him it wasn't easy to believe that in five minutes he could have you climbing the wall.

"What is phase two?" I asked, politely.

"The second phase," Tim said, "is when they start to disagree with me. Then they can't stand me. But if they get past that phase," he added quickly, "then they are my friends for life."

I forbore speaking for a moment. I got up and went over to poke at the fire so that the extreme effort I was making to speak lightly might not be so evident. After all, there were two of us in the house in phase two with Tim Bailey, the phase where you couldn't stand him. There was Kate in the kitchen, and there was me. But both of us were willing to make every effort possible to learn to live with that, since the rewards of knowing Laura and Suzy and Billy outweighed all other considerations.

There were many things in my mind. Many things I might have said or asked. About those people in phase two, for example; how did they get to phase three? Well, I could start with that, I supposed.

I cleared my throat. "Those people in phase two," I said. "Those people who can't stand you. Just exactly how do they get to phase three where they are your friends for life?"

"It's when they begin to share my point of view," Tim said.

There you are. Ask a foolish question and you will get a foolish answer. It happens every time. I might have known what Tim would have said. He knew no compromise, on any point of view. No compromise was possible, since Tim was always on the side of the angels, and do angels compromise? Tim was that fascinating and noble product of our time, the committed young man, the young man who was going to change the world and improve it if it killed us all. His being arrested with the anti-war demonstrators at the napalm gas plant had served notice of that. Yet I could not dismiss from my mind the feeling that we were responsible for him. We had made him. We were the times of which he was a product,

142

and if we could never get past phase two to phase three, at least we would have to learn to live with him.

Tim had just put the whole village through a test of moral conviction and I think it was safe to say that Kate and I were not alone in phase two. It was possible that the whole village was stuck there. It had all begun with the question of open housing.

This question had brought to our village, as undoubtedly it does to every community, a period of self-examination and soul-searching. No Negro families lived in our community. There were a few Negroes employed in houses, who came in by the day from Bellefield, a larger neighboring community. There were even one or two who lived in, and they were accepted as members of the community. The most famous of these had been Abraham, now dead. Abraham Porter had been a fine figure of a man, of Biblical stature, with venerable features and close-cropped white hair. He had been with the Wadsworth family for decades. The senior Wadsworths had died young, killed in an automobile accident. A maiden aunt had come in to bring up the Wadsworth children in their own house, and Abraham had stayed on, to help in that bringing up. He had still been there when young Bruce Wadsworth had gone off to the Army, and that year, on Father's Day, Abraham Porter had received a Father's Day card from Bruce in Vietnam. Word of this had gone around swiftly until the whole village shared the knowledge with a kind of secret joy, turning it about in their minds as if it were a jewel in the treasury of an ancient city. When Abraham died, not long afterward, the whole village turned out for his funeral, and those who couldn't get into the church stood outside to join in the prayer.

Then there was Penny Macomber, who worked for the Lowells, and lived there with her son called Mack, who went to the local school and sang in the children's choir. Mack was underfoot just like any other boy. No one thought about him.

But no Negro families lived in separate houses in our village, and Tim Bailey had challenged us about this. Were they excluded? Would they be welcome if they came? Did they somehow sense that they were unwanted? Were they, in fact, unwanted?

None of us seemed to know the answer to any of these questions. There was always the possibility that we didn't want to know, or didn't even want the questions asked, but it made all of us very uneasy. There was no platform for debate in our village, no town hall. The only time the whole village ever got together was once a year in the school to argue about school taxes. Tim had had his letter of membership transferred to our church, from whatever church he had previously belonged to (in a distant community from which some of our neighbors darkly suspected he had been escorted from town on a rail). It was there he challenged us, at meetings of the church officers who presumably represented the conscience of the community.

We had been away; I had been too busy later with the building of the new house to attend those meetings, but when I finally got back to them, in the spring, the beautiful spring of Cybele with the tulips blooming in our new paradise, it was just in time to be confronted by all of this controversy.

Surely we were opposed to discrimination? Of course we were. Well, we thought we were, anyway. At these meetings we said the usual, temporizing things, like "Maybe they don't want to live here." "Maybe they prefer to choose their neighbors, just as we prefer to choose ours." "We can't import them, can we?" "We can't force them to live here." And "Maybe they can't afford to live here."

None of this was good enough for Tim Bailey. If they

144

couldn't afford to live in our village, why was this so? Were they denied equal opportunity? Wasn't it perfectly obvious to anyone that they would prefer to live in our village rather than in the ghetto of nearby Bellefield? Tempers flared. Words were spoken. There was no ghetto in Bellefield. It was a decent, perfectly respectable neighborhood. But only Negroes lived there, didn't they? asked Tim Bailey.

At last Douglas MacClure, our minister, felt compelled to intervene. It was as foolhardy an act as running across no-man's land under the cross fire. Our church was Douglas MacClure's first church. He was young. He was idealistic. He believed in the goodness of all men. He typed up a statement of open housing on a long sheet of legal paper. It said, in effect, and in so many words, that in our community we were opposed to discrimination in housing on grounds of race, color, or creed. Mr. MacClure then went, like Martin Luther before him, and tacked this document, not on the door of the church, but on a wall just inside, in the vestibule, where it would be the first thing seen by anyone entering the church. From the pulpit, Mr. MacClure then asked the members of the congregation to put their signatures to this document, as witness to their stand on the question. With but one or two exceptions, everyone did.

This was not good enough for Tim Bailey.

How would anyone else know how we felt about this question if our statement was written on a piece of paper hidden away behind the closed door of the church? What significance had it there? Wasn't it our clear and present duty now to have this statement published in the local newspaper, even if we had to pay for space to do that, so that all our neighbors would know?

Again tempers flared. More words were spoken. Wouldn't such an act seem uncalled-for and ostentatious? Was it necessary to advertise our virtue? And if we were to come out with such a statement now, wouldn't it lead to the suspicion that we had altered an opinion previously held, when this wasn't the case at all? Wouldn't our neighbors in the larger community ask what "dialogue"—to use that currently fashionable word that young Mr. MacClure had brought to us from the seminary—was going on among us? Wouldn't they all be rather puzzled? Or suspect that we were involved in some sort of interior quarreling?

This was when Douglas MacClure fell into the quicksand. Of course Tim Bailey was right, he said. If we held such a point of view then it was obviously our duty, in these troubled times, to publish it for all the world to see. "I am for it," he said.

In the closed room where we were meeting, danger signals flared on all sides. The congregation of a church is held together, at any given moment, in precarious harmony. One theologian has said that no one could endure the smell inside the church if the smell of the world outside was not so much more odious. In the heated discussion which followed Mr. MacClure's statement, we were falling into two groups. On the one side there were those who felt that to advertise our point of view in the local newspaper was no serious matter, since our tolerance was well known. It would mean little; perhaps even be meaningless, but at least it would do no harm. The opposing group was more vehement. To publish such a statement in the local paper would be, they felt, absurd and demeaning. The church had no business taking a stand on such an issue. It was a matter of private conscience. The pulpit was not a platform for the dissemination of social opinions. The church a was a place of worship.

In other words, we were divided, and divisions in a church must be healed quickly before they lead to an irrevocable

146

breach. I had seen this happen before, and in every instance, no matter what issue was involved, or what its validity or outcome, the victim in the end was, inevitably, the pastor. The pastor had to go, always. It was almost as if, periodically, the redemption of man by ritual sacrifice had to take place all over again in the church at the local level. I did not want to see this happen to Doug MacClure. I didn't think any of us wanted to see this happen. He was the best minister we had had in years, perhaps ever. But if Tim Bailey divided us he would conquer us, and wreck our church.

When the meeting was adjourned, stormily, and without any conclusion except a motion to meet again, I rushed home so that I might telephone Douglas MacClure and speak to him privately. I told him of my thoughts. I told him that we could not afford to lose him. I told him that I thought I could promise that those who backed him in his support of Tim Bailey might get those who opposed him to go along on this issue if he would promise not to make such an impulsive decision again. We were imperfect beings. We longed for perfection, and we could be led toward that goal by persuasion, as long as he did not confuse us or frighten us by leaping ahead to make our decisions for us, without counseling us or talking with us first.

I think this was a little difficult for Mr. MacClure to accept, and perhaps he should not have, for to him the brotherhood of man was just around the corner, and might begin to function, say, next week, if we could just get the word to the proper quarters, and perhaps he was right. But in the end he agreed, and the rest of us agreed. We bought space in the local newspaper to publish our statement on open housing.

Nothing happened.

"But what am I going to do about Tim Bailey now?" Doug MacClure asked, hardly a week later, for that was not the end of it, not by a long shot.

147

"Leave him to me," I said, grimly. "I'll overcome him with love."

And that was how I came to be sitting in the late afternoon in the library of our new house with Tim Bailey. There was another issue to be resolved, even more sticky than the one before, and every day when he came home from his office, that pious foundation at which he was employed, where they were busy dispensing the money some scoundrel of a robber baron had made to the descendants of the poor wretches he had exploited, Tim came over to our house to bug me with it.

"But I don't see why you can't write me a letter," Tim said, over his glass of beer.

"Because you have given us no cause," I said, taking a rather larger drink from my own glass. "If you wanted your membership transferred to another church, that would be easy to do, but we can't write you a letter throwing you out of our church when you haven't done anything."

"I am not living up to the Christian way," Tim said. He spoke softly, giving me his warm smile, that look of modesty, or shared identity, which made so many men want to punch him in the mouth.

I heard the outside door of the kitchen slam, and I breathed a sigh of relief. I would be saved again for yet another evening. It would be Billy. Billy was always sent over to claim his father for dinner, and his reward for this errand was to be allowed to look at our television set for fifteen minutes. The Baileys had no television set. Tim did not approve. He did not want the corruption of our way of life brought into his living room. That was what he said.

I followed Billy's routine in my mind's eye, counting the moments until he would come to us in the library. He would first go to the refrigerator to get his private juice from his private part of the shelf, while he recreated for Kate and his own self-esteem some fictional part of the day in which he had supposedly over-achieved at something. Even though we had moved to the new house the kitchen was still Billy's domain, as was the seat at the head of the table at breakfast, simply because the old chief was too chicken to protest. On the shelf in the refrigerator in the kitchen, Billy's private corner, were the two jellies, as well as the fruit juice, and he would pour this into his private glass, which sat on a shelf of a cupboard low enough for him to reach, next to the breadbox, which also had space reserved for his private cookies.

I ticked off his progress and turned my eye to the swinging door of the kitchen, which I could see beyond the library, as Billy emerged, glass in one hand, cookie in the other. There were two periods of the day when Billy was clean. The first was in the morning, when he leaped from his house for the adventures of the day; the second period was at half-past five, when the record of the adventures of the day had been scrubbed from him, and he appeared at our door for his father. On his feet were sneakers rather too large, which flopped when he walked, and above those were clean socks, clean pants and a freshly laundered cotton shirt, out of which his shining face rose, topped by hair plastered down with a wet brush.

The routine was so unvarying that it was not necessary for Billy to speak. Holding his cookie in his mouth, he turned on the television set, ignoring us. Billy was instructed to look at one particular program, a virtuous program written and produced by certain virtuous and self-acclaimed educators, intended to capture the interest of the young while instructing them at the same time in some useful subject, such as the life cycle of a caterpillar. Billy never looked at this program. He turned confidently and skillfully to the nearest western, knowing that his father would be too absorbed in his own conversation to hear, and that I was too indulgent to protest.

"The Bible says," Tim said, leaning toward me, "that a man should give all he possesses to the poor and follow Christ, but I can't do that because I have a family."

"Bang! Bang!" went the television.

"I don't think that parable was meant for men in your situation," I said, raising my voice a little. "Or perhaps you should have read it before you got married."

"But I didn't," Tim said, "and I'm living a life just as corrupt as any man in our sick society."

I didn't particularly care for Tim's vocabulary in such areas, but I had given up protesting about it because I had never been able to convince Tim that maybe our society wasn't all that sick or corrupt, or that even if it was maybe we could do something about it. When I talked like that it merely meant, of course, that I was a fascist. Since I didn't like that word either, or labels of any kind, I shut up. Maybe I was a fascist. Why couldn't I just look at the television with Billy? What was happening to our country? Why couldn't we just be left alone in our house with our garden?

Billy had now arranged himself in his favorite position for looking at television. He was on the sofa. His head was erect at the lowest level of the back, his body flowed down and over the edge, and where it passed over the edge two inches of bare flesh were exposed, including his navel. He had eaten his cookie and from time to time he raised his glass of orange juice to his mouth, and drank from it, the juice seeming somehow to find its way down.

"Billy," Tim said. "Please don't sit that way. It hurts me just to look at you."

Billy flopped down on the floor without missing a single flicker of the television.

Billy was Tim's Achilles' heel. Tim loved his daughter,

Suzy, in the way that all men love their pretty little daughters, outrageously, and without judgment. The judgment, as well as his concern, was reserved for Billy. To be the father of a son is a privilege common to most men, and it is not only a relationship of great complexity, as I have said, but an experience so unique that no man has ever been able fully to explain it. It comes, and it is a fearful and a happy time, and it passes more quickly than one knows, since while it is happening one is too busy to think in terms of time, and when it is gone there is nothing left to show for it, not even a mark on the hand. It is one of the life experiences, perhaps the major one of its kind, which must be, like virtue, its own reward.

The virtue of fatherhood lay heavily upon Tim Bailey. It was the one area of his life in which he seemed to me to speak with any reason. He would say to me, "I don't want to do anything to hurt Billy, or to damage him. I could never forgive myself for that. Yet how am I supposed to discipline him? How can I be sure I won't hurt him or damage him?"

Tim Bailey asked me this question with such concern, with such anxiety, and with such an obvious desire for a reply that it was apparent that he did not know that this was one of the oldest questions of mankind. But you will hurt him, I thought, although I did not say this aloud. You will damage him in some way or other, as all men do their sons. Whatever hurt or damage I had done to my own son was very likely apparent to everyone but me, but whatever it was, I knew he would be discussing the consequences of it with himself in midnight soliloquies long after I had gone. A burden laid upon all men is the need to forgive their fathers.

For me, for better or for worse, all that was in the past. The fearful confrontations between father and son no longer took place in our house, but here now were Billy and Tim, and all

I could think to say to him was to repeat a maxim which some other older father had given to me when my own son was young. "Feed him, teach him manners and a respect for the law, and try to prevent him from hurting himself physically irreparably."

It was not enough for Tim. Nothing was ever enough for Tim, and I even wondered if it might not be through this arbitrary and unrealistic approach to life that he might in the end damage Billy. But Tim's young face, when he had spoken to me about that, had been drawn by concern. His eyes probed mine. What of other things? Like men of all time he wanted his son to be a man. What of ideals? Honor? Courage?

"Oh, you can't teach those things," I said. "He will have to find them in you."

It was a stopper, as it was meant to be, and Tim had been stopped. At least for a moment.

"Do you think Billy is a sissy?" he asked. "He whines. And he still cries sometimes."

"Sissy?" I had said. I could hardly keep my face straight. Billy almost never appeared in public without a gun. It might be a revolver, or a rifle, or the gun that shot death-ray pellets, but I think he felt undressed without a gun. Aside from the fact that this seemed rather strange to Kate and me, in the son of a man with such impossible ideals, didn't Tim realize its symbolism? They wanted Billy to have a "normal" boyhood, as Laura explained, in defense of the weaponry. Tim seemed to me at times demented, but certainly he was intelligent, and didn't he know that to certain unlettered and untutored men the possession of a gun was an affirmation of virility? Why had the backwoodsmen fought so hard against gun control laws if they had not felt their manhood threatened? Cam had once told me that in boot camp in the Coast Guard their gunnery instructor had taught them a jingle, to be helpful to those boys who had never had anything to do with a rifle, and persisted in calling it a gun. He stood before them, and grasping his genitals through his trousers with one hand, and holding a rifle in the other, he had said, "This is your rifle, and this is your gun. One is for shooting, and one is for fun." Didn't Tim remember that promiscuous boys spoke of the sex act as getting their gun?

"No, I don't think Billy is a sissy," I said. "And I don't think he ever will be. A Marine sergeant, maybe. A sissy, no."

And here we were now, the three of us, closeted in the library. Billy was on his stomach, his head propped up by his hands, absorbed in the television show he wasn't allowed to look at, where a band of Indians on horseback had surrounded a stagecoach and were trying to kill the occupants with arrows, who shot back at them with pistols. Bullets sang, arrows flew, horses screamed and fell, Indians gave their war cries, women shrieked.

"But I still can't see why you won't just write me a letter of dismissal," Tim said.

We had been all over this before. Practically everyone in the church had been all over it before. When Tim had written his letter to Doug MacClure, asking for a letter of dismissal, a special meeting of the officers of the church was called again.

And again words were exchanged and tempers flared. By implication, in Tim's definition, we were all failures as Christians. We all had families and responsibilities, one of those responsibilities being a concern for the poor. If everyone of us were to give up all that he had to the poor to follow Christ, then we would all be poor together, and who would be left to help any of us? Tim's smiling, soft reply, which did not turn away wrath, was to the effect that he was glad to know that we had learned to reconcile ourselves so successfully to the society in which we lived, and could continue to attend church in good faith, but he could not. If Tim wished to be expelled there were those among us, in our Philistine midst, who would have been only too happy to accommodate him, by force, preferably, but a letter we could not write. Tim, earnest and manly, blue-eyed and sincere, stood before us like Luther before the Diet of Worms. Perhaps Tim was right. Perhaps we were all worms. His stand was a judgment upon all of us. But we could not give him a letter of dismissal without reason. He could be expelled from our church only for certain stated reasons, for moral dismeanors, or violations of doctrine.

Couldn't he just stay away from church if he felt himself to be so unworthy? No, that would be too easy. Just as we had to advertise our virtue in the local newspaper, now we had to write a letter rejecting him.

And the worst thing about all of it was that it did make us feel like hypocrites. Maybe we were a little too comfortable. We were citizens of an affluent society. We really didn't want to be disturbed by unpleasant questions. We didn't want to give up what we had and submit ourselves, voluntarily, to poverty and hardship. What, in the name of reason, would that accomplish? Everyone began to search the Bible for texts in self-defense. Letters flew back and forth with thickets of Biblical references, and flew back and forth again with further references to fend off the references which had been used to attack the first. It could go on forever, and it threatened to become as meaningless and as doctrinaire as the medieval argument over how many angels could dance on the head of a pin. Angels or not, we had all danced quite contentedly on the head of our pin until Tim Bailey had come along to make us see how vulnerable we were, in what peril

154

we lived, how indefensible our standards might really be if we stopped dancing long enough to examine them.

"You want us to reject you," I said to Tim. "That's really it, isn't it?"

I was quite calm now in my stand on the whole question. During the heat of the argument I had made the mistake of going to Luke to look up the parable of the rich young man. In it, Christ had asked him first if he had kept the commandments, and the rich young man had said, "All these have I kept from my youth up." Well, that left me out. I would always covet something I didn't have, and there was at least one other commandment which had given me quite a bit of trouble at one time or another, although I don't think it is necessary to go into that here. Anyway, I would never be eligible for the final promotion to perfection. I could just hang onto what I had and enjoy my repentance.

Tim shook his head. "No," he said, "I just want a letter from you acknowledging that I am not a Christian."

"And acknowledging ourselves as Pharisees," I said. "No, that's a double play you're not going to catch us in."

At that moment the telephone rang. It would be Laura. Her messenger, as usual, had failed to watch the time, and the fifteen minutes had fled away. I picked up the telephone and spoke into it, over the din of the television. "They're on the way now, Laura," I said.

Billy was torn away from the television with reluctance. Father and son went back through the dining room to the kitchen. They would go home by the back door. A path had been beaten there by Billy and Suzy, from the back door of the Bailey house to the back door of ours, in their daily visits to the popsicle factory, which had also been moved, *in toto,* to its new headquarters. The fall before, Kate had officially acknowledged the existence of the path by planting bulbs along its sides, and in the spring the crocus had come up, in yellow and white and blue, and the daffodils, and the little sprays of grape hyacinth. It looked like the sort of path that might have sprung up in the wake of Persephone, when she made her way from the underworld in the spring.

Out on the path, Tim swung Billy up to his shoulders, where he perched proudly and possessively. He was a boy who loved his father with all the devotion of his small being. I felt a sadness looking at that little tableau. What would happen when Billy saw his father plain? Well, perhaps he would admire him with all the devotion of his grown being. If Tim seemed warped to us, it might be that way only in the slant of our own vision.

"Tim," I said. "Please get yourself down off that cross."

Tim looked at me, a little startled, and then he smiled. He turned and they made their way up the path, Billy's arms hugging his head.

CHAPTER ELEVEN

IT was when the fruit trees were in blossom that we learned that Laura Bailey was going to have another baby, and who wouldn't rejoice at that? Maybe Tim was a problem, maybe he was arbitrary and a zealot and a thorn in the flesh. Maybe he was a man obsessed. Still, as Kate said, Laura made such beautiful babies that perhaps they should be subsidized just to do that.

We were a little late in knowing about the pregnancy. Everyone, with the exception of Tim, was a little late in knowing about it. Deliberately. Long-limbed, fully-fleshed as Laura was, it was easy to carry the new child without anyone being aware of it for some time. "If I had told the children," as she explained to Kate, "they would have wanted to know about it every day. I could hear Billy saying, 'Is it today? Tomorrow? The day after?' " No, she had waited as long as possible to impart the news, but even so she had forgotten to take into consideration the boundless innocence of all. When she decided the time had come, she made the announcement as the family sat around the dinner table. "Children," she said happily, "we are going to have another baby."

157

There had been a moment of silence, of blank expression and raised spoons. Then Billy had spoken. "Which one of us?" he said.

We laughed at that, but no one realized at first, especially when the explanation was made, that this news was going to be received with something less than joy by Billy. Since there had been only one child in our house we didn't know anything about sibling rivalry. Since Billy the Chief was Number One in his house, neither did he, but he was going to learn.

But at least all other issues took second place for a while. There wasn't time to worry about how Christian or un-Christian anyone was until Tim got the nursery finished, a back bedroom upstairs in the Bailey house, which Tim was fitting out with shelves and cupboards. Now, instead of his coming over to bug me in the evenings, we heard the more cheerful sound of the hammer instead, or the whine of the power saw.

And Laura Bailey was never more in her element. In some way she brought the past back to me, for I had had a younger sister very like her. We always said that Jane had arrived on the scene about a hundred years too late. She would have loved being a pioneer mother, but since she had been denied these hardships she had to make up her own hardships as she went along. When she had a family she baked her own bread. "I don't know what they put in store bread," she would say ominously. "It still feels fresh in the store after it sits on the shelf for a week. Can you imagine what it must do to your insides?" Jane put her own additives into the bread she baked. Molasses, and wheat germ, and of course she used stone-ground flour, and the result was awful. It crumbled when you sliced it, and if you made a sandwich with it you had to eat it with a fork. But no one ever knew how it would feel if it sat around for a week, because it never lasted that long. Her children loved it, and they flourished.

We would have snapshots of them after various holidays, notably Easter, so that we could see the clothes she had made for the children. I think they must have bought their hats, and I suppose they had to buy their shoes and stockings, but everything else was run up on the old Singer in the bay window of the dining room. And there they would stand in the photograph, bursting with wheat germ and molasses, scrubbed with soap, not a synthetic chemical or additive in them.

Now I saw it all again in Laura Bailey. She baked her own bread, naturally, and when she did she sometimes sent us a loaf with Billy. It came in various flavors, called "rye," or "whole wheat," or "white." They were all just as awful as the bread Jane used to bake, and they bore no resemblance whatever to the rye, whole wheat, or white bread one bought at the supermarket, and whose additives I had become addicted to over the years. If you toasted a slice of Laura's bread it might hold together long enough to be eaten, and we would sit around telling each other how good it was for us, as it scratched its way down our throats.

Laura had a washing machine, in which she undoubtedly used soap instead of a detergent, but she had no dryer, and her laundry was hung outside. Tim had rigged up a hook and pulley arrangement in the back yard, with a line going from a post outside the kitchen door to a large ash tree at the end of the back lawn. There were some of our neighbors who would think that a wet wash was not the most commendable sight in a neighborhood such as ours, but Laura couldn't have cared less, and it fanned out from the back porch like brave banners of defiance. One of the more beneficial uses of the sun, that giver of life, was, according to Laura, to dry one's clothes in, and you could almost see the little defeated bacteria giving up and floating away.

A side benefit on laundry days was to see Laura hanging up the wash, as if she were performing one of the happy rites of a priestess. I loved to see her out there, her arms upraised to the clothesline, her figure in profile classically beautiful and pregnant, and dressed, as she usually was, in one of the long flowing garments which she probably made for herself, or which had been handed down in the family, like the dress in which she had been married, or the little christening gown in which her children were baptized.

There seemed a timelessness to life in the Bailey house now, and the days passed blissfully and serenely as the new life cycle began in Laura. Even Tim seemed at peace with himself for the moment. Thoreau has persuaded us that all men lead lives of quiet desperation, but perhaps he had never known the husband of an earth mother such as Laura. What crises arose during the period of gestation were coped with before they became desperate for anyone, and if further desperations lay beyond, which would not be coped with so easily, at least they did not have to be faced then. Meanwhile, life flowed on. Laura was teaching Suzy and Billy the difference between dirt and earth. Laura was teaching Billy, who was discovered taking coins from her purse, the value of money. Laura, after reading the surgeon general's report, was "helping" Tim give up smoking cigarettes. Laura was protecting her family from nuclear fallout.

"I do hate to be such a pest," she said one day at the kitchen door, lugging great cartons of fresh milk. "The paper says the Russians are testing again. Would you have room in your freezer to store some of this for me, just until the fallout has passed?"

Would she? Kate would have emptied our freezer for Laura

if that had been necessary. On Persephone's Path, where the crocus and daffodils had given way to violets and fern, not only Billy and Suzy, but Kate and Laura kept running back and forth, as if they had mislaid something, and while they couldn't remember just what it was, they thought they would recognize it when they found it. The flow of lemons and onions, of herbs and spices between our two houses was rather like the old traffic on the trade routes.

Kate had gone to the freezer in the corner of the kitchen while Laura talked. She was moving things around inside, from shelf to shelf. "You can have the whole top shelf here," she said to Laura. "We don't need nearly so much room now that there are only two of us."

"It will be only temporary, of course," Laura said. "I don't want you to crowd your things."

"But there is plenty of room here," Kate said. "Use it any time you like."

Laura looked stricken. "Oh, I wasn't hinting," she said. "Really I wasn't."

"There isn't anything up here but chicken stock I've saved," Kate said, "and bread, and I can move that to the shelf below."

"Well, I do plan to cook a lot of things ahead and freeze them before I go to the hospital," Laura said. "Mother has promised to come and stay with us for a month, but I'm going to save her until I get home from the hospital. Tim says he can cope, and I have a cousin, Helen, who is going to stay in the house while I'm in the hospital. Aunt Rose thinks it will be good experience for Helen in housekeeping, but I want to have as many dinners cooked ahead as I can."

I had been in the kitchen when Laura arrived, dawdling over a second cup of coffee and the morning paper. After helping her in with the cartons of milk, I had returned to my chair, my attention so riveted by this domestic drama that I found it impossible to leave.

"I should have thought of it myself," Kate said. "Just take this shelf as yours."

"Oh, that would be wonderful," Laura said. "I'm making some beef stew now, and when it cools I'll bring it over in freezer containers. The freezing compartment of our refrigerator is always so crowded with orange juice and things that I never seem to have any room."

"You could store bread in here, too," Kate said, as Laura peered over her shoulder into the freezer.

"Of course," Laura said. "I'll bake ahead. And soup. I could make soup, and I suppose I could even roast a chicken and freeze it."

"Oh, there's room enough for a small turkey," Kate said. "Turkey is always so good to have on hand."

Just then there was a tapping on the kitchen door, and there, peering through the screen, was Suzy. Whenever she could escape, Suzy would weave her way over to our kitchen. Billy was instructed to take care of Suzy while Laura was out of the house, but sometimes things went wrong with this plan, and Suzy would appear, speechless and beaming, running to our door, her tiny little feet put down so wildly and so impulsively from the ends of her wavering, spindly legs that her arrival was always something in the nature of a triumph, and she would smile, and wait to be gathered up, or she would encircle your legs with her arms, to catch her breath after her perilous journey, and to be rewarded with the orange juice popsicle, which was the goal of her expedition.

"Oh, Suzy!" Laura said, opening the door and swooping her up, taking a handkerchief from her pocket at the same time. Suzy was always in need of repair. Her smiling face was

162

smudged, her nose ran, her hair was disheveled. The problem was to get the thumb from the mouth, and the other hand untangled from the hair just long enough to restore everything to temporary tidiness.

"Billy is a bad boy," Laura was saying, smoothing, dabbing, straightening. "I suppose he's turned the television set on." For, lo, now the Baileys had submitted to television, even as you and I. With pregnancy, with imminent motherhood and the arrival of another baby, with all of the extra work that involved, even Laura had surrendered to the babysitter of the masses. "I told him to watch Suzy while I came over here, and he knows he's forbidden to look at television except when we allow him to look at certain programs—like that educational program he looks at in the evening at your house—but as soon as he's alone he switches it on to see if he can find some program with shooting."

"Awful," I said, clucking my tongue.

"Do you mind if I send Billy over with some things for the freezer when I get home?" Laura asked, as Kate went to the freezer to get the popsicle for Suzy. "It would be such a help to have more room in the freezing compartment of my refrigerator."

"Of course," Kate said. "Send him over."

I went to my study at that point, where I could shut the door and laugh. I thought of the great empire of China, which had survived over many centuries because instead of resisting its conquerors it had simply absorbed them. The Baileys had conquered us and we were absorbing them. Soon the whole house would be Bailey territory, and what would be wrong with that?

I sat there thinking of Laura and her definition of the difference between dirt and earth. It wasn't dirt you played in when you went out to scratch in the dust, or to dig holes in the play yard fenced in in the back. Dirt was man-made. It came from factory chimneys, or from the exhaust pipes of motor cars. It wasn't even dirt that you brought in on your clothes or your shoes, or smudged on your face. That was soil, in which things grew. That was earth.

"Everything we eat and grow on comes from the earth," Laura had explained to Billy and Suzy. "You must never call it dirt. Everything beautiful comes from the earth."

Indeed it did. Including Laura Bailey.

CHAPTER TWELVE

AND who could forget the morning when the new baby was born? It was shortly after sunrise when Tim appeared at the kitchen door, sleepless, pale, grinning, an old sweater pulled over his tousled head. "It's a boy," he said. "Everyone is fine. We're going to call him Matthew."

"Oh, my dear!" Kate said. "How wonderful! Come in! Come in! Have some coffee!"

Suzy and Billy were in tow, and it was from that moment, with Mother in the maternity wing, that we marked the complete, if temporary, demoralization of the Bailey household. Suzy appeared more schizophrenic than ever. Dressed in her nightgown, with her little feet bare, she danced up and down like a puppet whose manipulator had lost control of the strings. "Whee!" she screamed. "Whee!"

Billy had, as usual, dressed himself from his costumer's stores. Although it was a warm and balmy morning, he was wearing winter boots drawn over the pants of his baseball player's suit. Above this he wore a copy of the jacket worn by U.S. Marines in combat. On his head was a space helmet given to him recently by one of his indulgent aunts. It was a space helmet for the world of tomorrow, wired for light and sound, battery controlled. In front was a red light which blinked on and off at regular intervals, and on top of the helmet was a button. When this button was pressed, the helmet went "Beep-Beep!"

Billy's face was stormy. It was his avowed intent that morning to demolish his beloved father for having produced another son, but as slowly and as painfully as possible, by punching him in all of his more vulnerable parts.

"Thanks for the offer," Tim said to Kate, grunting and clutching his groin, "but Helen is fixing breakfast, and I have to dress to go to the office. Ouch! Billy, stop that!"

"Beep-Beep!" went Billy.

"Isn't it great to have a baby brother?" I asked Billy, unaware at that moment of the cause for mayhem. "What do you say about that?"

Billy glowered at me. He punched his father in the bottom. "We may have to throw him in the garbage," he said.

I saw the light. Sibling rivalry had reared its ugly head and doom was in the air. It was like the opening of a Greek tragedy. The young prince, the chief was threatened. The usurper must be overthrown.

"Come on, kids," Tim said, herding the rabble toward the door.

"I'll be here," Kate said. "I want to do anything I can."

"Thanks," Tim said. "Ouch! Billy, stop that!"

"Beep-Beep!" said Billy.

It was Friday. Fortunately, as everyone kept saying, the weekend was at hand. With any luck, Laura would be home with Matthew on Tuesday. Meanwhile, as Laura had said, Tim would cope. It was the most preposterous statement of the century. A man less able to cope could scarcely be imagined. He was the sort of man one could imagine, as a

166

pioneer, holding the horses while his wife had her baby at the edge of the field before returning to the plow. Nothing could be done until she got back on her feet.

Cousin Helen, a lovesick adolescent, mooned at the television, interrupting herself now and then to whip up batches of peanut butter sandwiches. In the evenings the frozen dinners disappeared from the top shelf of the freezer, and were presumably consumed, although since Laura had failed to write instructions on the sides of the containers, they may have been eaten with ice picks.

By day the Bailey yard filled with neighboring children, who appeared as soon as the word of social collapse had gone out, to dance and shriek the hours away, just as the French revolutionaries had done when it was learned that the king and queen had lost their heads.

At intervals Kate went out to sweep the Baileys in for periods of resuscitation. Suzy now resembled one of those small children whose photographs are distributed by international welfare organizations to plead the cause of absentee adoption, usually with captions such as, "Won't Someone Save This Helpless Child?" Billy, in swimming trunks and undershirt, with a bath towel pinned at the shoulders, was Superman, although a sort of Superman in reverse, bound on flights of destruction. The shrieking of his victims made hideous the hours.

Tim tried to remain calm. Brought inside with the others, he sat with me, as before, in the library, although now, as a welcome change, talk of carpentry took the place of social issues. Tim had finished the nursery, but when it was finished, he and Laura both realized that now they had no guest room. Tim knew just where a guest room could be added. They would build it off the end of the upstairs hall in back, and below it Tim would have the workshop he had always wanted, with a place of residence for his power tools. It wouldn't cost too much. Tim could do the inside finishing himself, with his trusty power tools.

"If only I could have a cigarette," he said, getting up and jamming his hands in his pockets, and pacing back and forth. "I miss it so much more with Laura in the hospital, but I can't bear to have the kids on my back."

I knew what he meant. I had seen the performance. Laura's way of "helping" Tim give up smoking had been to train the children in separate roles. When Tim lighted a cigarette, Suzy burst into tears and flung herself at his feet, and Billy shouted, "Cancer!" clapping his hands to his mouth in shock.

"It was too much," Tim said, shaking his head. "It's easier to give up smoking than to put up with that."

"I'll get us a beer," I said, standing up.

Through the door in the living room, which was now also Bailey territory, as well as the library, I could see that Kate had set up an emergency nursery school, using the supplies from the toy cupboard in the corner. The toy cupboard was a mahogany cabinet, once used as a bar and a storage place for liquor in younger, less responsible days, but which now served to house an accumulation of toys and games for children of younger friends whose friendship we wished to maintain. Of these toys the most successful, as we had learned, were broken toys; a little car with only three wheels was much more beguiling than a set of Chinese checkers with all its marbles. It took usually less than five minutes to spread the entire contents of the toy cupboard over the living room floor, although somewhat longer than that was required to gather it all up again.

Here, on a carpet of shattered Tinker Toys, dismembered dolls, and broken cars, popsicles were served after grace, toast with two jellies before, and lemonade flowed in between.

Back in the library, over our beer, the pleasure dome of the new addition to the Bailey house rose in Tim's addled mind, while over at the Bailey house itself Helen sobbed over shadow tales of unrequited love while she stuffed herself with peanut butter sandwiches. So the long weekend passed.

But sometimes things have to get worse before they can get better, and the really critical phase in the Baileys' domestic crisis began only after Laura had arrived home from the hospital with little Matthew. Superficially, everything seemed well. Grandmother had arrived. Cousin Helen was dispatched. Order seemed restored. Billy arrived at our house as usual at breakfast time. Even before Laura had gone to the hospital, the length of these daily visits had grown. He had seemed to sense even then the new and alien presence in his own house, so he worked to establish even more his new and alien presence in our house, where his primacy was uncontested. He stayed on and on and sometimes he had to be threatened with exile by Kate if he didn't heed his mother's pleas to come home for lunch.

Now Billy seemed to bring with him unspoken undercurrents, ominous threats of internal disorder. In this new atmosphere the relationship between Kate and her gentleman caller became rather like the relationship between Louis XIV and Madame de Maintenon, with intransigent stubbornness on the one hand, and domestic piety on the other.

"But you must go home for lunch, Pet," Kate would say. "You know that I would love to have you here, but your mother wants you to come home for lunch."

"I'm not going home for lunch," Billy would say.

The telephone would ring. It would be Laura. "I'm sorry Billy is being such a pest," she would say. "Tell him to come home for lunch."

"Tell her I don't want any lunch," Billy would say.

169

"You must go home for lunch."

"I won't."

"You wouldn't want to hurt your mother, would you?" Kate would say.

"Why not?" Billy would say.

"Goodbye," Kate would say.

"Dumb old Mother," Billy would say, slamming out of the door.

Rumors of horrid tales began to filter to us from the Bailey domain. Words were exchanged. Tears were shed. There were scenes with such lines as, "I hate you." And even one episode which ended with, "I wish you weren't my mother!"

The accumulated tension worked up to a rather predictable climax one evening at bath time, as reported to us later by Laura, who knew she had done it all wrong, knew that even at the time, but felt powerless to behave otherwise. Laura was bathing Suzy, in one of those palace scenes where everything is thrown open to the public, and people come and go at will in the nude. Billy, waiting his turn at the tub, amused himself by shooting everyone with his water pistol, filling it with the soapy water from the tub. Suzy shrieked and giggled. From his crib in the next room, Matthew wailed. Laura, soaked and dripping, soap in her eyes, pleaded for mercy. Billy was relentless. With a villain's laugh he hopped about, gunning everyone in sight.

"Billy, stop!" Laura said. "Stop at once!"

Billy's answer was to aim a jet of water at his mother which caught her full in the face. She burst into tears.

"If you don't stop this minute I am going to run away from home and never come back!" Laura said.

"So long," said Billy.

It was too much. Sobbing, Laura fled down the stairs. She flung herself at Tim, who was helping Grandmother with

170

dinner by carrying the dishes to the table. "I told Billy that I was going to leave home if he didn't behave," she cried. "And he said, 'So long!'"

Father Tim saw red. Dishes banged onto the table. Up the stairs he flew, two at a time. There was the repeated sound of bare hand on bare bottom, but there was no sound from stubborn Billy.

"Just for that," he said, glaring at his father, "I'm not going to have a bath tonight."

"Oh, yes, you are," said Tim.

"Oh, no, I'm not," said Billy.

Billy was carried to the tub, rigid, his knees drawn up, his arms clasped around them, looking like one of those small and angry stone figures which once lined the steps of Aztec pyramids. He was dumped into the tub, still rigid. The exposed parts were scrubbed vigorously. He was dabbed dry and carried back to bed, still rigid, knees still drawn up.

Clearly, something had to be done.

By the dawn's early light we could see that steps were already being taken. The Bailey car had been pulled from the garage, and beside it on the lawn the camping gear was spread out. Tim was rolling the tent, and in a moment Billy came dancing to the back door.

"We're going camping!" he said. "We're going to meet Uncle Jack, and Bobby, and we're going to take the canoe!"

"How wonderful!" Kate said.

"I think I'll have one popsicle before I go," he said, "but maybe I'll have my toast with the two jellies first."

He rushed about the kitchen, getting the bread from the breadbox, putting it into the toaster, getting the jellies from the refrigerator. He was wearing denim pants and galoshes. The fringe on his Daniel Boone shirt bobbed up and down.

On his head was the space helmet. The red light went off and on.

From the kitchen door I watched Tim. I wanted to go help him when I saw him carrying the canoe from the garage, balancing it over his head, but I hesitated to do so. Sometimes it is best to stay out of things. There was something very solemn in his manner, and I wasn't at all sure that I wanted to know just who had made the decision that sent Tim and Billy off to the wilds.

"Goodbye!" said Billy. In one hand was the toast with the two jellies. In the other was the popsicle. At the door he carefully balanced the popsicle on the toast. He opened the door. He pressed the button on the top of his head.

"Beep-Beep!" he said, dancing away.

A lonely peace settled upon us. Now in the morning instead of receiving her gentleman caller, Kate went to call on Laura and Matthew, and I had glowing reports about that.

"He's simply darling," Kate said. "It's just as I said. Laura does make such beautiful babies."

"Don't you think Tim might have had something to do with that?" I said.

Kate smiled. The Mona Lisa couldn't have done it any better.

But Tim had the last word. We didn't know the whole story until after it was all over, but the camping trip had been memorable. It had been a sort of combined virility test and premature puberty rite combined, where men and boys go out to pit themselves against the elements, and emerge victorious. It had rained nearly all the time, Laura said. "Tim took the sick leave that was due him at the office for the trip, and it was a wonder they didn't all come down with pneumonia." And they never washed at all. "As far as I know,"

Laura said, "they didn't even wash the dishes." They took the canoe downstream, and they portaged back upstream, and they followed trails, and they saw animal tracks, and even, as Billy insisted, Indian tracks. They made fires, and cooked their food, and at night they crawled into their grubby sleeping bags and slept soundly in their own dirt. (Not to be confused with earth.) They were up in the country where men were men, and there wasn't a solitary woman within gunshot.

And in what an odor of triumph they returned! They stomped into the house, bringing it all with them, the ruddy cheeks and the smells, and the transparent bravado of scorn for all the comforts of home they were so obviously glad to get back to.

"And how is Little Brother?" Tim asked, restating the nature of primogeniture, which Billy had learned to accept in his absence from home, and by which acceptance he had learned to come back to it so happily. "Did you take good care of baby brother?"

"We tried to," Laura said, falling gratefully into the solemnity of this newly acquired knowledge.

"Well, I suppose the men had better bathe first, before they go in to see the baby," Tim said.

He had done it. Tim had done it. He had taken a small, disgruntled boy away from the house where he felt supplanted by the arrival of another, a threat to his own importance. And he had brought back a man in the making, with room enough and love enough in a heart suddenly enlarged by pride for all the little brothers in the world.

We learned all this from Laura, when Little Brother was brought to call on us, shortly after that, with his court. It was Matthew's debut into the great world, and he made his appearance carried by his mother like a precious jewel, to be shown and exhibited when layer after layer of fine wool and linen had been unfolded, and his rosy little face was revealed. We made the usual efforts to try to express our joy at seeing him. Laura smiled happily. "My only problem now is to try to keep Billy away from him," she said. "Billy seems to have brought back a cold from the woods, and now he wants to hug Matthew all the time and kiss him and play with him."

Billy and Suzy had been ensconced in the library with lemonade and cookies, where, for a blessed interval, they were permitted to look at a television show of their own choosing.

"I do hope Matthew doesn't catch Billy's cold," Laura went on, caressing the little cocoon in her lap, from which two tiny fists emerged and waved about. "But it's really a lost cause," she said. "You can't win. I left Billy alone for a moment today with Matthew while I went to answer the telephone. I asked him to watch the baby, but I told him he was not to kiss him or hug him or breathe on him, because I didn't want Matthew to catch his cold." Laura could scarcely control her laughter. "And do you know what he told me when I came back to the room?"

"What?" we said.

"He said, 'I was very good, Mother. I watched Matthew, but I didn't hug him or kiss him or breathe on him.' Oh, he was very pleased with himself. He said, 'No, Mother, I didn't do any of the things you asked me not to do. I just let Matthew lick my lollipop.' "

We laughed together. The chief had done it again. I excused myself and left the room and went to the kitchen. At the telephone there I dialed the Baileys' number, thinking, as I dialed, of those people, presumably a small confraternity, who had gone beyond phase two, where they couldn't stand Tim Bailey, and had somehow reached phase three, where they were his friends for life.

Tim answered the telephone. He had just come in from the office.

"Tim," I said. "Could you come over and have a beer with me? I think I'm going into phase three."

CHAPTER THIRTEEN

AND so began The Summer of the Baileys, one of the most joyful periods of our life. There was not even a suggestion of a cloud on the horizon. It was like one of those golden summers which precede, as historians are fond of telling us, world wars, or other disasters. Glorious day followed glorious day, in an eternity of pleasure. We had planned no vacation trip that summer, since we were still busy settling into the new house.

At the Baileys' the new addition was going up. During the day professional carpenters were there, and the sound of their hammers in the summer heat had a sort of distant familiarity about it, as if the sound of hammers were always a part of the memory of summer happiness. In the evening, after an early dinner, Tim would be up there himself, and on the weekends his power saw was set up outside the garage door, where he was busy framing cabinets and building storage drawers and closet shelves. Suzy and Billy ran about with visiting children as swiftly and as aimlessly as butterflies, lighting now and again for a moment, and then up and away again; they were at the kitchen door for a popsicle, they were swooping across the terrace like swallows, they were giggling under my window until it was impossible to sit at my desk. We liked our house all on one floor, but in one way that might have been a mistake, for how was it possible to do any work in a study whose window looked out at eye level at summer?

Well, if we weren't going away for a summer change of scene, we could create our own diversions at home, and for my afternoon project, when my work was finished, I chose the weeding of an old herb garden, still on the property we had retained for ourselves. In one misguided year mint had been planted in the herb garden, not merely one mint, but mint of several varieties, as if one plague weren't bad enough, and now the mint threatened to take over completely. It became my self-imposed task to root it out and let grow in freedom again the thyme and the sage, the tarragon and the chives, the beebalm and the lavender. It was a fragrant task, in a terrain I shared with the bees, with whom I practiced coexistence.

Would that the effort had been more widespread. Indeed, for peace of mind, it was best not to look at the morning paper, with its burgeoning quota of wars and domestic violence. We tried, in the early days of that summer, The Summer of the Baileys, to keep the world and its problems at bay. For her summer project, Kate began with Laura. When Grandmother left the Baileys, she kept a practiced eye in that direction. After all, earth mother that she was, young as she was, healthy as she was, there was a limit to the endurance of everyone, although, as Kate would sometimes remark darkly, young husbands are not always aware of that. Tim just took for granted the boundless energy of his wife. The laundry, the cooking, the bread baking, the care of Suzy and Billy, and now the care of a new infant; they were all simply a part of life. "It keeps her out of mischief," Tim would say. But

Kate watched, and because she was never really happy when she was not doing something to help someone else, she soon founded what I called "The Kate Wallace Rest Home For Exhausted Mothers."

The Kate Wallace Rest Home For Exhausted Mothers was centered in our guest room with its bath. The long windows of this guest room at the back of the house looked out on privacy, into the woods, where ferns grew, and the jack-in-the-pulpit was to be found in the spring. The Rest Home was one of those projects which Kate threw herself into, renewed by whatever effort it required. The double bed was made up with fresh linen and flowered pillowcases. Fresh flowers were arranged on the tables. Beside the bed on a table was a thermos jug of ice water and a glass, and on the turned-down bed a fresh nightgown was laid out. When the exhausted mother was admitted, most often on a Saturday, when Father was home to care for the children, there was a rigid routine to follow. The telephone in the room was unplugged. No messages were allowed. A hot tub was prescribed first, a long soak in scented water. Luncheon was served on a tray, and in the afternoon there were fresh magazines to read, and only when the rag-tag and bob-tail of children and Father appeared at the kitchen door, with desperate pleas, was the now somewhat less exhausted mother permitted to dress and go home.

Word spread of the Kate Wallace Rest Home, and mothers other than Laura came to its facilities, but it was imperative that the Rest Home not be booked for Tuesdays, for on Tuesdays Kate did her day for charity. The charity project was called the Thrift Shop, and I don't think Kate and her friends had had so much fun since they were little girls and played house. It gave me pleasure too, of a guilty sort, for on Tuesdays I was alone in the house, and as much as I loved Kate and our life together, I also enjoyed the days of respite when peace and silence fell over the house in soft, restorative layers.

Since the Thrift Shop was all for a good cause, it made it acceptable to enjoy its workings. And I will try to explain how it worked if I can, using as an example one particular Tuesday, for on that Tuesday new chords were also heard in our lives, such as introduce themselves into symphonies, and develop later to form themes, which gradually transform the work.

On this Tuesday the telephone rang shortly after nine, just after Kate had left for the Thrift Shop. I was in the kitchen, having a second cup of coffee, enjoying the quiet of the house, an enjoyment which I must say in all fairness would predictably diminish in proportion to the time Kate was away.

The call was from Tim Bailey. He wondered if we couldn't have lunch that day. I responded with pleasure. Of course. I would be delighted to have lunch with him. But his call surprised me. We had lunched together a couple of times before, on Saturdays, during that month after Matthew was born, when Grandmother was in residence at the Baileys. We had gone to a country restaurant back in the county, newly opened, a pleasant, simple place called The Steak House, with a bar and few tables, where hearty food was served to local businessmen. We had enjoyed ourselves in a way, I suppose. Tim needed a break, as he said, from women and children and diapers. I hadn't yet made my way to phase three, where I learned to accept Tim as he was, and I didn't find the conversation very entertaining, with its predictable talk of the sickness and corruption of our society, and the words like fascism and racism. I had tried to deflect the talk into other channels when I could, and the food was good, and I had a martini while Tim drank his beer. We had spoken of doing it again, but this was Tuesday, a work day.

"Is something wrong, Tim?" I asked.

179

"No," he said. "Not exactly. I just thought it would be good to have lunch again at The Steak House. How about one o'clock?"

"Fine," I said. "I'll be there." Doubtless the mystery would resolve itself later.

I drank my coffee, thinking about the Thrift Shop. It had all begun when someone had either given to Kate's committee, or rented to them at a very low price, a small, empty store in the poorer section of our neighboring village, Belleville. Here everyone was encouraged to bring his household surpluses, in the way of extra clothing in good condition, kitchen utensils, dishes, books, alleged objects of art, or whatever it was that cluttered the shelves or closets. These objects were in turn sold at minimal prices, ostensibly to the less privileged of the neighborhood in which the store was located, although, as we shall see, this was not necessarily the case. The proceeds from the sale of these objects were then divided between two or three worthy causes, notably a play school where the children of working mothers could be left for the day. A perfect scheme, and indeed it worked perfectly, but for one puzzling result, which I hadn't yet been able to figure out, but which filled me with awe, and made me feel that perhaps some government finance officer could be profitably called in for instruction on how to balance the budget without raising taxes. The worthy causes and the play school received a handsome stipend at the end of each month or so, and yet the number of objects which left our house was balanced by the number of objects brought back in. The right hand didn't seem to know what the left hand was doing, but the right hand couldn't care less, and everyone was having a wonderful time.

Between Tuesdays the house was gleaned for discards. As Tuesday approached there was generally a point at which I was called in for consultation and approval, but this was purely a polite gesture, and both parties were aware of that. The closet of the guest room had been chosen as the collection depot, and on some day when the guest room was not functioning as the Rest Home For Exhausted Mothers, the articles would be brought out from the closet and spread out on the bed and hung over the chairs.

That morning, for example, the following objects had left our house. (1.) A crystal cigarette box which we had been given as a wedding gift, which a careless bump had chipped on the bottom. "You can't really notice the chip from the top," as Kate said, "and someone will be very glad to have it." (2.) Two summer dresses in perfect condition, which the owner thought might drive her out of her mind if she ever had to wear them again. (3.) One copy of *Crime and Punishment,* by Feodor Dostoevsky. In moving from the old house to the new it had been discovered that, unaccountably, we owned two copies, and surely one *Crime and Punishment* was enough for any one house. (4.) A raincoat left by a person unknown who had failed to claim it after two years. (5.) A Mexican tin mask of a god with his tongue sticking out, which everyone was very tired of looking at. (6.) A collection of Navy whites which the owner was very reluctant to part with, although he could never, under any circumstances, ever get back into them again. "Now, dear," as Kate said, "be reasonable. The Smithsonian really won't want them." (7.) Six iced-tea spoons. (8.) An antique apple corer. (9.) An ashtray stolen from the Chateau Frontenac in Quebec. And (10.) a box of unused Christmas cards bought from the newspaper boy, which no one had ever had the courage to send out.

Thinking of all this my eyes finally focused on the desk at which I was sitting in the kitchen, where I had carried my cup of coffee when the telephone range with Tim's call. It was Kate's work desk, a pretty desk, an old one which we had bought at auction many years before. The auctioneer had said that it was the sort of desk once found in Victorian households, where the butler or someone sat to do the household accounts. It seemed fine in the old house, and rather surprisingly it looked good in the new house too. It was small and it had a roll top, with pigeonholes inside. On top of it, fitted into the small brass rail which ran around the back and sides, were cookbooks, and if you looked there you could always tell just what province of cookery had captured Kate's fancy for the moment, for there was room for only a part of her collection of cookbooks. There was a field guide to the birds, too, kept there always for instant reference, and on a corner of the top was a little sea gull, carved from wood and perched on a cork, a gift from her gentleman caller, Billy, after a weekend trip to Maine.

Suddenly I looked at all of this as if seeing it for the first time and I wondered if it would be possible for someone, an archaeologist, or a sociologist, to construct from this evidence just what sort of woman sat at this desk, that fascinating, often exasperating, and always complicated woman who was my Kate.

The roll top of the desk was up, and there, with my coffee cup, were pencils, and a wooden file box of her mother's recipes, and there were stray picture hooks, an extra pair of reading glasses, the china finial broken from the top of a sugar bowl waiting for repair, and an envelope which contained a single brass screw. And then there were the lists.

It is my feeling that lists are to women what flight is to birds. It is the way by which they float or propel themselves over the rocky way. My mother once admitted that sometimes at the end of a day she wrote things on her list which she had done, but which had not been written there, just for the pleasure of crossing them off. On Kate's desk there were lists like fallen leaves or drifts of snow. There were grocery lists and and shopping lists and lists of things to do, some of them addressed to herself, and some to poor Ernest, the village handyman. Ernest was community property, his time so valuable it was measured out in half-days. We owned Ernest for one of those precious half-days each week, a period often fraught with tension and elements of the love-hate relationship. For Ernest there was only one way to do anything, which was his way, and many a promising employer-employee relationship had been broken on those shoals. Our relationship with Ernest was like marriage. We couldn't live with him and we couldn't live without him. The lists for Ernest were headed "Ernest" in a firm hand, underlined, evidence of the futile but lingering hope that some day the writer's will might prevail, although it never did, and under this heading were written such arcane and baffling instructions as "flats," "path to P.O.," "rose hole," "mixture for trench," and "do something about clock." There was, in fact, a sequence of lists which went from "do something about clock," to "see if clock can be moved," to "see if clock can be repaired," which surely contained a drama of clashing wills and perhaps even violence, which might have been material for a story if I had wanted to write it, which I didn't.

I put all of the lists back neatly where I had found them. I sat for a moment looking at the little sea gull perched on his cork. No archaeologist or sociologist could have recreated Kate from the evidence he would find there. She was too elusive for that. She was as unpredictable, as mysterious, as enchanting and enchanted as any woman. I carried my coffee cup to the sink and went back to my work. Already the house had begun to seem too quiet, and I knew how relieved and happy I would be when Kate came back.

Kate came back from her joyful duties at the Thrift Shop

for a quick lunch just as I was putting on a clean shirt and a tie to go to meet Tim at The Steak House. She carried a shopping bag, and with childlike delight, and the gleam in the eye of a woman who knows she has found a bargain, she exhibited for my delectation and delight, the following objects, which she had bought that day to bring back home to us:

(1.) A copy of *Carry On, Jeeves,* by P. G. Wodehouse. "I remember how much you used to like him," she said. "I thought it would be such a nice surprise." (2.) A heavy silver bracelet inset with turquoise by some unusually clumsy tribe of Navaho Indians. (3.) A collection of tin things that were either cookie cutters or the things you used to cut out tea sandwiches with if you wanted fancy shapes. "My tea sandwiches always look so *ordinary,*" Kate said. (4.) Half a dozen linen napkins monogrammed in such a baroque manner that no one could be quite sure what the original owner's initials were. "They could be anyone's initials," Kate said, "so why not ours?" (5.) A pair of baby booties, unworn, for the gift drawer. The contents of the gift drawer, a drawer in an old chest which sat against a wall in the hall, could have provided, on instant notice, a complete table for the local rummage sale. (6.) A skirt of imported linen. "It cost only fifty cents!" Kate said. "And I do hope I can find out who brought it in, because it's just my size, and I'd love to know what else she would like to get rid of!" (7.) A brass postage scale, which was just what I had always wanted, but not very much. And (8.) an ashtray stolen from the Café Rotonde in Paris.

I expressed my delight at her taste, my admiration for her cleverness as a shopper, and my awe at her business acumen. I kissed her, and went off to lunch with Tim.

184

CHAPTER FOURTEEN

At these luncheon sessions of ours I found a very different Tim from the man I found at his house, or even in our library, as if he showed me one half of a personal dichotomy, a sort of Dr. Jekyll and Mr. Hyde personality which left me rather unbelieving, or confused, as if he were playing a trick on me. I wanted to say, "Oh, come off it, Tim." Or, "You're not really fooling me behind that mask." I was reminded, not very happily, of the old days when I had been stuck in phase two, and resented him, and had withheld from him my full friendship, before I had learned that the two men were equally part of the same man, and that if one were to be happy with one man, the other had also to be accepted.

There were times, of course, when these two persons were visible at his own house, unexpected moments. Although we no longer spoke on the question of open housing in our village, or of the hypocrisy of some Christians, this was because Tim had directed the full passion of his nature to a resistance of the war in Vietnam, his commitment to that cause growing with the escalation of the war. Strange people came to the Bailey house, people who, when seen, looked oddly familiar in a disturbing sort of way, as if one had seen them pictured in an alien, public context, such as marching with protest signs, or being dragged by police to police vans, and indeed this was quite often the case. We had been invited, for example, to Matthew's baptism, which was of course not celebrated in our church, that edifice for Philistines, but in the front room of the Bailey house. The front room of the Bailey house, which had once harbored the Harmon antiques, and where on cold evenings a fire had burned decorously on the hearth in a scent of lavender and lemon oil, now had that somewhat barren look of the houses of the families of today whose children are brought up in full participation in family life with their elders, and where there are no off limits. In such a circumstance furnishing is rather a process of elimination than of decoration, and so in the front room of the Bailey house, which I had not been permitted to see for so long, there were merely chairs and a sofa, with a large, low round table in front of it, equally suitable for the playing of games or the serving of refreshment.

This room, on the day of Matthew's baptism, had a secretive, conspiratorial air, not unpleasant, but of the sort one might believe appropriate for the hidden meeting place of a sect of heretics. Among the invited guests was a Roman Catholic priest, as well as a former Roman Catholic priest. There were also a Quaker and a Protestant clergyman of some unstated denomination. They were, if we had known, the scarred veterans of many a confrontation with the forces of law and order, and they shared a smiling but mildly demented appearance, as if theirs was a different reality from the one we knew. Matthew was baptized by, I think, the Protestant clergyman, but the others spoke quiet prayers invoking improbable blessings, in an atmosphere that at once seemed to be that which we associate with the early Church, when the communicants met

186

in the catacombs or in private dwellings. One had the feeling that the forces of evil and opposition were there outside, not at any great distance, but recognized for what they were when they so often went unnoticed by others, and were resisted, and held at bay. It was a chilling feeling for what would normally seem a happy occasion, and it was a relief when Laura brought in fruit punch and cookies to serve, in her everyday manner, from the low round table.

But now we were at The Steak House for lunch. The Steak House at noontime was a hearty, noisy place, with the local businessmen out in force, sometimes divested of their jackets and having a glass of beer with their food. The whole atmosphere was one of camaraderie and a sense of the physical appetites, much as in a painting by Breughel. Tim struck a rather somber note in the midst of this, but it was he who had discovered the place, and favored it. He was waiting at the bar, holding a glass of beer, and he brought it to a table and we sat down. I ordered a martini and when the waitress came with the menus we ordered what we always had, the open steak sandwich.

Tim was very depressed. The news of the war was anything but cheerful, and he looked about the room, at the laughing men, slapping each other on the back, touching each other, and in his smiling way he wondered quietly how they could seem so uninvolved. The casualty list had been published that day and it was higher than the week before, but there was also talk of something called a peace feeler, and this depressed Tim even more.

"Every escalation of the war has always been preceded by a peace scare," he said, in his way of inverting words or their meanings, so that I would have to listen carefully and proceed carefully, in order not to be caught out on a limb.

"Peace scare?" I said.

"This war is no accident," Tim said. "What frightens me most, I think," he added, "is not that our leaders, our military and political leaders are such liars, but that the people are so eager to believe them. I think it must be that deep down in their hearts the American people don't want to face the truth about themselves any more than the German people did."

We were back there again, in that alien world, that no-man's land where I could not walk with Tim, or seem to communicate with him even if I tried to walk with him. It gave me the same chilling feeling I had felt at Matthew's baptism, of forces of evil held at bay, which were either realities I could not see, or hobgoblins called up by Tim to frighten me.

"Why do you speak of the American people," I said, in an effort to divert the conversation to terms more reasonable to me, "as if you were not one of them?"

"I'm beginning to feel that I am not one of them," he said. "Our society has become so corrupt, we have gone so far along the road of absolute materialism that I'm beginning to feel that I could not keep up even if I wanted to. But, after all, we do own sixty percent of the natural resources of the world, and we have to protect our interests, don't we?"

"Oh, come on, Tim," I said. "This is your country as much as anyone's. Whatever you feel is wrong with it, don't you think that can be corrected through our traditional democratic institutions?"

"And we have the type of leaders we have," Tim said, interrupting me, "we have the type of leaders we have because most Americans will not willingly give up the type of life that makes material values more important than human values. Of course we aren't any different from any other nation of the world, except that we have more power and ability to look out for our materialistic interests than they do. But if they had it, they would."

188

"What do you want to do, Tim?" I asked. "Resign from the human race?"

There was a momentary lull in the noise of the room at that moment, and what I said came out clearly, and we laughed at that, as others turned to us. Food was being served. Our steak sandwiches came, and soon the sound level in the room had risen again as the men settled down to the serious business of eating and talking.

"You are a family man, Tim," I said, speaking in what I hoped was a matter-of-fact tone. There were times when I reminded myself that I was just about old enough to be Tim's father, but I didn't want him to think about that because I enjoyed his friendship, and if I took on a paternal tone I was afraid that I might jeopardize this, so I tried to sound merely practical and not avuncular. "You've got to bring up your children in the society in which you live, and if you don't like that, then you must do your best to change it."

"But I'm beginning to think that can't be done any more," Tim said, looking at me over his plate. "That's what worries me. I think it is too late."

"What do you mean?" I asked.

"Well, as I said," he began, "this war is no accident. It isn't the President who is the villain. We are the villains. This war is the logical result of our brand of imperialism and capitalism. In order to extend our way of material life and maintain it, we must exploit the Negroes at home, and develop a foreign policy which will see in any change in the world a threat to our way of life, and go out to subdue that change by force."

I put down my knife and fork. I could not eat. "You say such extreme things, Tim," I said. "You make such sweeping generalizations. Certainly you know that I am opposed to war, and that I am opposed to any exploitation of Negroes. All men of good will are."

189

Tim took another bite of steak. "You men of good will haven't got us very far, have you?" he said.

"Please don't make me angry, Tim," I said.

Tim favored me with his most beguiling smile. "I don't want to make you angry," he said. "If you can live with it, that's fine."

I took up my fork again in silence. I thought of our new house, so comfortable for us. Of the life Kate and I had there which we loved so much. How privileged we were. We lived so far from the world's concerns. But we had worked hard to get there. We had known a depression, and many hardships, and I had fought in a war for my country, and I liked to think that perhaps we had earned a little serenity and happiness at this time of our lives. Tim's probing concern was like a worm in the apple of our happiness. Were we wrong? Was there something we were not doing? Was our happiness and our withdrawal from the arena of life, in which we had once performed our duty, a kind of evil in itself?

But, come to think of it, what had Tim done? If everything was so hopeless, what had he tried to do to change it?

"What have you done to try to change things?" I asked.

Tim shrugged. "Everything," he said. "I've marched. I've protested. I've signed petitions. I've written letters. It does nothing."

"But surely you can't give up so easily," I said, a little angry now on two scores, I think, for his having made me doubt my purpose, and for his own youthful impatience. "You can't expect to change the world overnight," I said.

"You can't expect to change our country at all," Tim said quietly. "Dissent is permitted now. They've finally been convinced about that, even at the Pentagon. Dissent is permitted. But it is absolutely meaningless. It does nothing to influence any policy, either here or abroad. We speak, but we are not heard."

"What do you want to do, Tim?" I asked.

"I don't know," he said. "The alternatives seem to be getting fewer. About all you can do is go to jail or leave the country."

We finished our food in silence.

I must have looked a little troubled when I arrived back home, because Kate, working with her trowel, got up to ask me what was the matter. She had been relieved of her duties at the Thrift Shop by some other worker eager to play house, and she had returned to her gardening.

"I'm worried about the Baileys," I said. "I don't know what is going to happen there. Tim is very upset about the war. About everything."

"Hasn't it always been that way?" Kate said. She was setting out a border of seedlings of some kind along the driveway, and she went back to that.

I went into the house. A cloud passed over the sun and the sky darkened for a moment. The Summer of the Baileys seemed threatened.

CHAPTER FIFTEEN

OF course Tim Bailey was not the only man in town concerned about the war. We were all concerned, even if we were
not in agreement in our concern. We had our hawks and our
doves, although no one knew in exactly what proportion. In
our village we still stoutly defended the right of every man
to his own opinion, although we had wondered in the spring
how this division of opinion might affect the annual cere-
monies at the flagpole on Memorial Day.

Of all the days of celebration in our village, Memorial Day
seemed in some way to be the most personal, possibly because
so many of us had come to the village as veterans of World
War II. The flagpole had already been there, it was true. It
had stood there before the Civil War, on the triangular plot
of grass which served as our village Common. It had been replaced once in our time, for there had been a rather alarming
moment, perhaps eight or ten years before, when it was discovered that the flagpole was rotten to the core, which seemed,
in some way no one dared express, an unspeakable symbol of
moral or social decay which must be immediately excised.
The pole had been taken down and a new one raised, at the

same site, where the granite boulder stood at its base, bearing the bronze plaques on which were listed the names of the young men of the village who had died in past wars. There were those who said that the new flagpole was merely the most recent in a succession of flagpoles which had gone back to the victory pole raised at the end of the Revolution, but no one knew this for sure, not even Elder St. John, the self-appointed head of the Flagpole Committee. It was Elder St. John, with his pink face and white hair, who got up early each morning on national holidays to raise the flag, and who lowered it at sundown. On Memorial Day there were a lot of men, young and old, who wanted to get into the act, and they usually succeeded.

Our village was the point of assembly for the parade, as if we were the headwaters of a stream which then flowed on, gathering tributary streams, to the villages of Belleville and Rivervale and beyond. There were those of us who considered this a rather doubtful honor, since it meant getting up earlier than usual on a day one might have slept later than usual. But none of us had ever missed it. We were always there, gathered at the flagpole before nine, in warm weather, or cool, in rain, or shine. There would be freshly made wreaths waiting on tripods, those indestructible military wreaths looking as if they too had been made of bronze, and around them various functionaries were gathered; the head of the American Legion with his medals and his overseas cap; the head of the Ladies Auxiliary of the American Legion, in her cap and cape; our minister and the local priest; the chief of police, his men lined in military ranks behind him, beside the ranks of the volunteer firemen in their dress uniforms and white gloves. The fire engine was the proudest object of the parade, polished until the gleam of its brasses hurt the eyes. Later in the day small boys would be allowed to ride on it, but they could only admire it wistfully from afar, free of their fingerprints, until after the parade. There was a military honor guard, of course, with rifles, and pacing nervously somewhere at the edge of all this splendor would be the local citizen chosen that year to deliver the Memorial Day address. He would not speak until the Brownies had arrived in uniform, taking their place in the ranks beside the Girl Scouts, the Boy Scouts, and the Cub Scouts. When all were in place word was somehow carried back to the school, where the school band waited, and then in the magnificence of their new uniforms, they marched to the flagpole, playing, somewhat shakily, and with mercifully less than seventy-six trombones, a Sousa march, with tassels and the baton of the conductor flying.

The ceremony itself was rather brief. The minister or the priest spoke the invocation. The address was given, with varying degrees of success, depending upon the public-speaking qualities of the speaker, and the vagaries of the public address system, which had a way of going off into ear-splitting whines, perhaps of criticism, at unpredictable moments. When the address had been given the various wreaths were brought forth to be placed at the base of the granite boulder with its bronze plaques, and at this moment the chief of police went to the road which passed through our village to stop the traffic. The honor guard was called to attention, and upon order shattered the quiet of the countryside with a volley of its rifles, always a signal for small boys to scramble for the spent cartridge cases. In the echoing silence that followed, the bugler of the school band played taps, an assault upon the emotions which no sentient man could hear without a sudden spurting of tears. Then the closing prayer was spoken, by the minister or priest who had not prayed at the invocation, and the parade gathered its forces and was up and off down the road, flags flying, trombones blaring, led by the resplendent fire engine, to new glories at Belleville and Rivervale and beyond.

Those who had gathered did not disperse so quickly. It was a time of greeting, of visiting with old friends and neighbors not often seen, of catching up on news of families. Memorial Day in the spring of that year had been no different. There were those who had hinted that with the increasing confusion and dissent over the war, many might stay away. The prediction was groundless. Everyone came, even if a sense of full participation seemed muted. Jim Hunter had been chosen to give the address. It was a good choice. He was a teacher, intelligent, without sentimentality, who spoke to us of our honored past and the history of the day itself, without reference to the divisions among us. As he spoke my glance had gone about the crowd, checking who was there. Bob Crawley was there, and he had been a Green Beret, but he was home now, safely, for good. And Tom Meadows' head stuck above the crowd, and he was our pacifist, or intended to be when he was given the chance. Tom had always been a boy the village claimed with possessive pride. His father had died when he was young, and Tom had been fathered by every man in town. He had been an active, happy small boy; a healthy older boy, athletic but gentle, courteous but tough. Now, like so many of his contemporaries, he wore a beard, and standing there fair and tall and broad of beam he looked rather like Poseidon, with his wide, bearded face, and his faded blue eyes. His draft board had been unable to reclassify him, since he was not a member of any religious sect which might qualify him for pacifism. He waited now for his number to come up, and when he would be taken to the induction center he would not take that forward step. He would be led away, presumably, to the office of the district attorney. It did seem to me, however, that the sight of Tom Meadows, all the fit one-hundred-and-eighty pounds of him, might well strike terror into the heart of any district attorney, and I felt rather sorry for him, whoever he was. Tom remained calm.

"I don't know what's going to happen," he said, when we met him as we circulated among the crowd to speak to friends. "I'll just have to tell them that I can't go to this war. I think this war is wrong." He smiled. He was seemingly unconcerned. The village was not quite so unconcerned as he. Responsible men had talked to him, on both sides of the question. There had been evening bull sessions, with those Tom called his peers, his friends who were all faced with the same decision. There had even been a meeting, I had learned, called by Tim Bailey at his house, where Tom was counseled by the faithful there, in that atmosphere of the early Church. He would have legal counsel if he needed it, brought to him through this underground of dissenters.

It had seemed not at all strange that he stood there with us that morning, to honor those who had died in the name of their country. His fair head stood higher than those near him, and he held it with his customary pride. Who was there to fault his patriotism, since what he proposed to do he would do also as a loyal American? He had recited the allegiance to the flag with the rest of us. He had bowed his head in prayer. Time would be his judge. Certainly we were not prepared to be.

"I wish I could do it in some other way," Tom had said. "If I have to go to jail it's all right with me, but I wish it didn't all have to be so dramatic."

The volley of shot was fired; the bugler played his taps. Behind my closed eyes I saw, as I always did at this moment, the smiling face of Jimmy Bolton, the first of the men I had trained with to die in World War II. He had been a practical joker. At night in the barracks he liked to short sheet beds, and he was the sort of man who thought it was funny to dash a glass of cold water on the back of a man in a hot shower. He had gone down on a torpedoed tanker in the North Atlantic. None had survived in that sea of burning oil. "Goodbye, Jimmy," I always said in my Memorial Day prayer. "God bless you."

These memories and reflections, the division among us, the unhappiness and frustration in the air as the war continued, the threat to The Summer of the Baileys, all these I tried to push aside for as long as I could. But Laura herself began to bring bits and pieces of their unrest and concern into the house with her.

Laura rarely had the time to make a proper call, or even to sit down when she came. Only very seldom, when Kate made an issue of it, did they sit down over a cup of tea. Most of the meetings were spontaneous. Laura would come to borrow something, or to return it. Possibly she had something to store on the Bailey shelf in the freezer, which, even after the birth of Matthew, had remained in fee simple in Bailey territory. On occasion, when I opened the door of the freezer, for a tin of frozen orange juice, perhaps, forgetting, I would stare with disbelief at gallons of strawberry ice cream, bought at sale, or stacks of cartons of frozen spinach, and once I had even gone so far, in my absent-mindedness, as to cut into one of Laura's crumbling, uncontaminated loaves of bread before realizing my error.

On these spontaneous visits Matthew would be carried on Laura's hip, where he seemed as happy as any baby Hottentot in that primitive position, and while they went about various tasks, or stood at the door, protesting their lack of time for visiting, Laura would catch Kate up on the drama, so that we had episodes of it like those in a television serial. Tim now

197

spoke of quitting his job. It was not that he objected to the work he was doing. At the foundation they were, naturally, on the side of the angels, but even there Tim could not prevent the office from withholding his income tax for the federal government, and the fact that this money was being used to subsidize an unauthorized war, any war, began to bear like a weight on his conscience. For Laura, a loyal wife, a woman who loved her husband and shared his opinions, but whose viewpoint was, of necessity, constrained by the responsibility of three small children, the distress was doubled. Her eyes would grow round with horror and indignation as she echoed Tim's words. "To think of our money being used to kill people!" she would say. "To bomb villages! To drop napalm on innocent women and children!"

No, it was too awful to contemplate, and she felt as horrified as Tim did about all of it, but what were they to do? Her face wore a look of perpetual concern now, as she made her trips back and forth, with freezer containers, with a gift of cake or cookies, with a recipe given or borrowed. Kate's sympathy flowed out to her. But it stopped short of Tim, and it became increasingly evident that she was never going to make it to phase three.

"He should have thought about these things before he married," Kate would say, moving about her kitchen with righteous indignation. "He has a family to support, and that should and must come first. Look how hard Laura has to work, while he sits around mooning about his conscience!"

I did not take issue with Kate. I forbore from saying that the war in Vietnam had not been going on when Tim was courting Laura. It had been a very different country in those days. But still, Tim's first duty was to his family and to his children, and so even I ventured to speak to him about this, in one of our late afternoon sessions in the library.

"You once told me you didn't ever want to hurt Billy," I said, "and I'm sure you don't want to hurt Suzy or Matthew either. If you give up your job, what will happen to them?"

"We could always go on welfare," Tim said, with his gentle smile, his tone of irony. "We could let the Great Society support us."

"You know you wouldn't do that," I said.

"How do you know that?" Tim asked. "Isn't it possible that it would hurt my children less to live on welfare, than to live comfortably in an economy based on war? Think how unfair it is! Think how arrogant and corrupt it is to withhold my tax, and then not consult me or anyone who represents me on how it is to be used! Is that a democracy?"

How could I answer that? What was the answer? I could only repeat what I had said before, that administrations did not last forever, and that it was his country, and if he did not like what was going on, he must work to change that.

Tim shook his head. "They do not listen. How can you bring about change when those who are in power will not listen? It is not my country," he said. "The country is the Pentagon. It is the military-industrial complex."

We were at an impasse again.

But meanwhile summer went on. Threatened or not, tainted, it seemed, like a bruise on the side of a ripening peach, summer went on, with its vacations, and its fetes, and its parties. It was at one of these that we learned what had happened to Tom Meadows, when he had reported to the induction center.

His mother could hardly speak from her laughter. We had stopped her as she made her way across the lawn from one group of friends to another at a garden party, because we knew that Tom was due to be called up, but we had not heard what happened.

"Oh, he couldn't bear to have anyone know!" Betsy Meadows said, holding one hand with the other, to steady her cup of punch while she shook with laughter. "They turned him down! It was two hours after he came home before he would even tell me about it. He just went to his room and shut the door."

"They turned him down!" we said, incredulous. They had rejected mighty Poseidon, with the fair beard and the milk blue eyes! Why?

"Because," Betsy said, gasping, "they say he has flat feet! He never complained of it himself, but it seems he just played too much basketball, or too much baseball, or too much something, and they said it would just get worse if steps weren't taken, and now he has to wear corrective shoes, and he would just like to crawl into a corner and hide!"

It was the sense of relief that made Betsy laugh, we knew that. How much better to have him at home with his flat feet, than in jail with his betters.

"Poor Tom," I said. "You mean he never even got to make his stand? He never even got to make his statement of principle about the war in Vietnam?"

Betsy shook her head. "No," she said. "He never got beyond his flat feet. The doctor turned him down. They just sent him home."

What an irony it was. All of the talk, the meetings and the conferences, the discussions with his peers, the counseling of the protesters and the dissenters had come to nothing. As with Tim Bailey in a different context, he was not heard.

But Tim Bailey in his different context finally made up his mind to do something about not being heard. One day he came home from the office, and he had quit his job.

200

CHAPTER SIXTEEN

It was a few days before we knew this, or at least had our misgivings confirmed. There was an unusual amount of activity at the Bailey house. The new addition, with its guest room above and its workshop below, had not yet been finished. The outer siding and the trim were not all in place, but now it was apparent that an effort was being made to bring it all to completion. The power saw came outside again to be set up in the driveway, and we could hear its whine, and the sound of the hammer, but the surprising development was that Tim was there, all day, with the workmen. Billy and Suzy came less often to our door during those days, now that they could be with Father, but there was one day when Billy came dancing to the back door to announce happily that they were going out to lunch. Mother was going to Grandmother's for a visit, and she would take Matthew with her, but Suzy and Billy, oh, treat of treats, were being taken to the diner for lunch!

Luncheon at the diner was a hallowed custom which had its origins in those days after Matthew was born, after Grandmother had departed, when sometimes the whole thing seemed too much for Laura. On weekends when Tim was home he was merely another dependent, to be housed and fed, surely the last thing in the world Laura needed. As noted before, Tim was something less than useful around the house. There are men who can help out in family life, and there are men who cannot. It would have seemed, superficially, that surely the construction of a baloney sandwich would not be beyond the reach of a man so clever with a power saw, but apparently this was the case, and on days when Tim was at home and utter chaos seemed at hand, salvation was to be found at the diner at the crossroads, where the truck drivers stopped. It was a place of earthy camaraderie between patrons and waitresses. There was also a jukebox turned on fortissimo, which thus made it the only place in the world where Billy and Suzy did not have to be told to be quiet, since they could not possibly be heard even if they shrieked. While they reveled there with Tim, amidst the peanut butter and jelly and french fries, Laura was permitted a little oasis of silence at home where she might make some effort to regain her reason.

It was on this particular day, after Tim had gone off with Suzy and Billy in the Volkswagen truck, that Laura came to us with Matthew, dressed for travel. They were in the little Volkswagen, the one Tim drove to his office. Laura looked pale, and harassed, but she moved with her customary competence. She carried Matthew to the door, and this time she allowed herself a moment to sit down with Kate in the kitchen.

"Tim has quit his job," she said, in a matter-of-fact tone. "We are finishing the house so that we may rent it. We must then find a place where we can live on that rent, and since I cannot imagine where that would be, we will probably have to leave the country. I am going to Mother to tell her about that, so she will be prepared."

"Leave the country!" I said. I had seen Laura come to the door, pale, harassed, competent, and I had gone to see what was the matter.

"Tim will not pay his federal income tax," she said. "When he told them at the office that he had joined the tax refusers, they had to let him go. With all our deductions, the income from rent on our house won't be enough to require us to pay tax."

"But how can you live on that?" I asked.

"The alternative is for Tim to go to jail," Laura said, "and what would I live on then?"

We could say no more. Laura gathered up Matthew and left us. The Volkswagen skittered on the gravel as it whirled out of the drive.

Kate and I could not even speak to each other. Kate went back to whatever it was that had occupied her in the kitchen when Laura came, and I, knowing that I could not go back to my desk, went out to my summer task in the herb garden.

I saw now that I had lost. Fresh spears of mint came up everywhere, as if merely encouraged by my efforts to weed them out. It sprang up in the beds of tarragon and chives, in the thyme and the sage, the beebalm and the lavender. With sudden decision, I went to the tool shed for the spade. It would be hard work, and not pleasant, but the whole garden would have to go. The roots of the mint had traveled beneath the flagstones put down to serve as walks, in imitation of a medieval herbary; I had to lift those out and set them aside before I could begin my task. The earth was not unyielding. It had rained two days before, but the tangled roots of the mint formed a great mattress to resist the spade. I dug them out in great tangles, with a feeling of something like anger.

We had let ourselves be taken again. We had let ourselves love, and now we would be alone again, and that would hurt. My love for the Baileys, for Billy and Suzy and for Laura and Tim, had entangled itself among all of the other impulses of my life, springing up in places it had no right to be, and to root it all out it would be necessary to lay waste to the whole garden of my feelings.

It wasn't fair. I heard myself saying that to myself, aloud, but I could not ask myself what wasn't fair, for I would not have known the answer. I had cautioned myself in the beginning. I remembered that. I was not to let the Bailey family serve as substitutes for Cam and Nancy and little John, but I had done that. I had invested what feeling I had to give in them, but it had happened slowly, without my realizing the extent of it. We had been so happy, but happiness is mortal, even as we are; it never lasts, and it dies, and growing older is a process not so much of giving up things as of having things give one up instead.

Or was it something larger than that? Tim Bailey was not taking his family away from us to follow a new job, or for any caprice; he was leaving us in protest of a way of life. "You men of good will haven't got us very far, have you?" he had said to me with his gentle smile, that day in The Steak House. Well, if I had failed as a man of good will, along with all of the other men of good will, to bring social justice and peace to the world, then I was being punished for my failure, for that which I had found good was being taken from me.

"You'll wear yourself out, dear," Kate said. She had come up from behind to me at my task and I had not seen her until she was there. She had her hands folded in her kitchen apron. "Come in for lunch," she said. "I've made some sandwiches and tea. We can sit on the terrace if you like."

Her face was thoughtful, and there was not sadness there,

but a kind of resignation. Besides, she would have a scape-goat, and a scapegoat always helps.

"I cannot imagine what Tim is thinking about," she said, as we walked back to the house. "Doesn't he know what he is doing to his family? Doesn't he have any regard for Laura and the children at all?"

I did not answer, for these were questions I could not answer. The mint in Kate's heart would have to be uprooted too, but she would have to do it in her own way.

CHAPTER SEVENTEEN

THE next few weeks were busy ones for the Baileys. Tim had his hands full. He had to finish the new addition. He had to bring the old house up to repair, so that it could be rented. The lower step of the front porch had to be replaced. A part of the soffit under the eaves had rotted away, and this had to be cut out and replaced. There was scaffolding everywhere, and paint pots and ladders, while inside Laura was busy going over things, packing, discarding.

At intervals all of this activity came to a halt when visiting counselors arrived, to sit in the front room of the Bailey house to discuss the possibilities and alternatives of exile. Just as Tim had made us aware of the existence of the heretics and dissenters in his living room, now he made known to us the existence of others who had taken his stand on taxes, a group known to each other in that definition, which we had also just learned, of tax refusers. These talks began with the premise that Tim would not risk a prison sentence. He could not do that to his family. He had Laura's support in his decision, which helped, but it carried certain conditions in the setting of their plans. They would not have the money to go very far or live with any luxury, but she did not want to go to any place so alien that her children's American heritage would be threatened. She would not go to Mexico, for example, where they would have to make their way in a foreign tongue. They could scarcely live anywhere in our country on what income they would have, which certainly did not displease Tim, but there were exiles in such outposts as Canada and the Maritime Provinces, where life was possible on marginal means. They would not be alone there, either. There were other Americans who had gone ahead.

Tim took time off from his labors to make a scouting trip. One of the visiting advisers had recommended Nova Scotia. There would be fewer American exiles there, year round, for work opportunities were limited. When most young draft evaders went to Canada, they went to cities such as Montreal or Ottawa, where it was possible to find work. But since the Baileys would have some income, they might like it better in a village on the sea.

Tim left, in the little Volkswagen. He might be gone for as long as a week. In his absence, would we keep on eye on his family and his house?

Indeed we would. It was our last opportunity to spoil them all. Every indulgence was granted. Suzy and Billy were permitted to look at television, any program, unsupervised, until they became hypnotized, and had to be led away, with glazed eyes, for naps. It was a part of the afternoon tea party routine, when Laura came finally to stay and visit, with Matthew sleeping on the sofa beside her, while she and Kate talked and talked, as if they would never have time to finish what they had to say to each other. Laura, that loyal and loving wife, had begun to respond to the upheaval of their life as if it were an adventure. It would be almost like living on an island. To get to Nova Scotia one took a ferry from Bar Harbor in Maine, across the open sea, to Yarmouth, on the tip of the peninsula of Nova Scotia. Once there it would be a village life. A simple life. Think how good it would be for the children!

And when Tim returned, the eagerness, the concept of exile as adventure grew. He had found the village for them. He had found the house for them. He had found a way of life for them, away from the corruption of home. The village was a fishing village on the sea. The men went out for lobster and herring. The whole village supported itself on this industry. The house he had found for them stood near the salt marsh in wide fields, with an apple orchard behind it. They could rent it for almost nothing. It had no central heating, of course, but then the winters weren't severe there. They were not even as severe as our winters were, so the story went, because they were near the sea, and in the sea the Gulf Stream swept by, to modify the rigors of winter. Why, they didn't even build foundations under the houses in this magical village, for the freezing never went deep enough to make that necessary! As for heating, there was a wood and coal range in the kitchen, and there were pot-bellied stoves in the lower rooms, with vents in the ceiling to carry the heat upstairs.

And why, I wondered, did this perfect house stand empty, to be rented for almost nothing? I could see it all in my mind, with the eternal fog rolling in, and the endless days, as empty as the rooms in the house with the pot-bellied stoves, in that bleak part of the world where the range of color in the visible spectrum seemed diminished the further one went north. I had seen Halifax during the war, that gray city of dark stone, dripping in the fog.

But I could be wrong. Oh, I must be wrong. It was beautiful, Tim said. There were only about a dozen families or so in the village, and that meant one had to learn to live on one's inner resources, and wasn't that all to the good? Also,

208

in practical terms, exile would be possible there, without the annoyances or restrictions sometimes encountered in other countries. No work permit was required, for one thing. The village had no carpenter. Tim could take his power tools, and set up a little shop there, and augment their income with local work. My heart sank. He had got himself down off the cross, but now Tim was living the story in reverse. He was biding his time in his father's house with his carpenter's tools.

"You mean it really is as simple and wonderful as that?" Laura asked. "We need no visas? No passports? No permits of any kind?"

Tim shrugged. "They want you to come," he said. "They need workers. They encourage you to come."

"And school?" Laura asked. "Is there a school?"

"Of course there is a school," Tim said. "A one-room schoolhouse for the children of the village."

"I can take supplemental things," Laura said. "I must get busy with that right away. I can go to the library and ask them about that. Or perhaps I should call the board of education. They must have a list of recommended things." She looked at Tim, and her face lighted, reflecting his happiness.

Now that plans were complete, they could hardly wait to be off. The sound of the hammer and the whine of the power saw filled the air from dawn to dark. Barrels arrived from the moving company, for Laura to begin to pack her china for shipment. They would have to pay duty on what the moving van carried on the ferry from Bar Harbor to Yarmouth, and so she must select with care as she packed and take just what she needed and no more. The bare necessities. The rest she could store in the attic, or leave for the tenants to use.

The bare necessities. Socrates had once said that the wise man should conduct his life so that when the city was besieged he could leave with all of his possessions on his back. The Baileys were content, it seems, to follow Socrates' advice.

As for the tenants, they now materialized, at least for the Baileys, although we did not see them. And perhaps we never would, Laura said, in a tone meant to be reassuring. At least we would see very little of them, for they both worked in the city, and they would commute each day.

Persephone's Path would be choked with weeds.

CHAPTER EIGHTEEN

THE Baileys were to leave for Nova Scotia in the evening, and on that evening we would have a picnic for them. The picnic would be many things. It would be a farewell. It would be a party. It would also be a great help to Laura, for when the van was packed and gone they would be temporarily unhoused. They could have dinner at the diner, but, no, Kate said, this was out of the question. While the van moved ahead we would have an early picnic supper, and then the Baileys would take off in the Volkswagen truck. The small Volkswagen car had gone. It had been sold, disposed of, in that elimination of all the things unnecessary to life which the wise man practiced when the time had come to flee. The Baileys would spend the night somewhere on the road in a motor hotel, and on the following day they would rendezvous with the moving van at the ferry at Bar Harbor.

The preparations for the picnic gave us something to do while the Bailey house was being emptied. Kate loved a picnic. She always said it took longer and was more difficult to prepare than a dinner party at home, but I don't think she ever said this as any form of complaint. It was just an observation. She loved to cook. She loved the kitchen, and I was even tolerated there as scullery boy. I was given certain assigned tasks, and as long as I performed them competently and stayed out of the way my presence was welcome.

Any honest picnic began with chicken salad. The chicken was simmered the day before and cooled overnight in the refrigerator in its own broth. My task was then to skin the bird, and take the meat from the bones and cut it up. But I must be careful to follow instructions. A sharp knife was mandatory, and I must on no account cut the pieces too small. A generous nature manifests itself in all ways. Kate despised smallness in anything, including the size of the pieces of chicken in a salad, and so I had learned to do this in her way. Kate cut the celery; she made the mayonnaise. The proportions of the final ingredients were a mystery which only she knew, and my duties ended short of the assembly of the salad, which then went back into the refrigerator to be stored until the last minute.

Meanwhile the cooked, diced potatoes for the potato salad had been marinating in hot beef broth, to be drained and also dressed with mayonnaise. Wedges of tomatoes went into Mason jars, with oil and vinegar and chopped fresh basil. There were hard-cooked eggs to be deviled. There were hearts of celery, and black olives and green olives, and there would be, of course, a chilled bottle of dry white wine. When I was a boy and we had gone on family picnics to the picnic grove, we children used to run swiftly by other tables, to see what other families had brought for their picnics, but this curiosity had disappeared from me after I had married Kate, and if we went to a picnic grove I never wanted to know what others had brought, for I knew that at no other table would there be food as delicious as at ours.

For picnics, it was also my task to pack the back of the

station wagon, and this I did with careful deliberation, taking my time, because once I had forgotten the ice bucket when we had gone deep into the woods on a summer picnic, and this was an omission not easily forgotten or forgiven. Packing the back of the station wagon for the Bailey picnic was a complex and complicated task, not merely because there were five Baileys, but also because of the comforts and luxuries with which our age of affluence had burdened us. There was one basket alone for the china and the silver and the glass. I had made the decision about the china, long before, for how would one dare eat such peerless chicken salad from a paper plate? The silver was actually cutlery of stainless steel, but we had glasses of various kinds, since not only would there be wine, there would be a jug of martinis, and bottled fruit juice for the children while we drank them. Then there was another basket for fruit and cookies, and the crackers and potato chips to be eaten at cocktail time. Only after that could I turn my attention to the ice bucket, and the insulated carrier which held the cold food. And of course we must not forget the insect repellent, and the blankets to sit on if we decided to picnic on the grass, and the cushions to sit on if we decided to eat at a picnic table, and the Kleenex, and the napkins, and the tablecloth. Those picnics we had gone on when I was a boy had been carried in one basket; a large basket, it was true, which one or another of us was sometimes permitted to help carry, but life in general had been more spartan. I didn't think we wanted to return to that, but I had been thinking, now that the Baileys were turning their backs on it, that we had become slaves to our ways of affluence.

There had been the incident of the electric blanket just that week. The nights had grown cooler as fall approached, and I had wakened in the middle of one night to an unaccustomed coolness. My electric blanket had ceased to function. In a way I blamed Kate for the indulgence of the electric blankets. It was she who had brought them into the house. She resented, she said, using her own energy to warm a bed when she was already tired. Like Eve with the apple, she had led me from the innocence of honest woolen blankets, and now I too was hooked. I had taken my defunct electric blanket that very day to the appliance repair ship, appalled at the thought of warming my bed with my own precious energy. I had walked up to the technician there like a man, and said, "My security blanket died in the night, and I am lost without it." The repair man seemed not at all reproachful. He was as hooked on affluence as any of us. The shop around him was filled with gadgets, not one of which would go with the Baileys to Nova Scotia, but which most of us now found indispensable. He sent me away redeemed, with a new heat control for my blanket.

We were hopeless. We didn't even care.

The evening of the Baileys' departure was memorable in many ways. It had been a beautiful, golden day of autumn, warm, and in the early evening the air was still and dusty. In the Bailey driveway the Volkswagen truck stood packed to within an inch of its capacity, and for the picnic trip the Baileys came with the picnic itself, wedged into the station wagon. We had decided to go to the bluff over the river. There was a public park there, with wooden tables and benches, and pits for broiling on cast-iron grills. We knew that no one else would be there. After Labor Day the flow of picnic parties from the city came to an abrupt halt, as if a decree forbidding picnics had been passed, or as if some ancient migratory instinct had asserted itself. No matter how beautiful the weather was, no matter how prolonged the season was, no one came, and we had learned to wait until this time of the year to go to the public parks for a picnic, when they seemed to belong to us.

We chose a table overlooking the river, under the shade of gum and maple trees, the leaves now gently falling, gently changing color. They rustled dustily underfoot, and Suzy and Billy ran through them to set them whirling. We brought all the comforts for the picnic from the car, making several trips to be sure we had everything, and then we settled down in the midst of it. Kate and Laura busied themselves at the table, and I had a martini, while Tim had his beer, for now more urgently than ever, it was imperative not to cultivate expensive tastes.

It was all, as one might imagine, rather uncomfortable and sad. The mosquitoes were out in force. They had apparently never heard of the mandate against picnics after Labor Day, and since there were so many of them, and so curiously few of us, they charged in battalions in kamikaze formation, the shock troops sacrificed to the insect repellent so that the others might get through, and as we fought them off I found myself thinking that it was the only time in my life I had ever been grateful to mosquitoes for anything, for that night they did provide us with a diversion. Still, I talked, simply because I could not be silent.

"Things can change in a democracy," I said. "Things could change so fast that you might be back in a year."

Tim looked doubtful. "It would have to change a very great deal," he said. "We're so committed everywhere that it isn't going to be easy to undo."

"And you don't think you could help change that?" I said. I said it almost hesitantly. It was a question I had asked so many times, and always with so little success that I knew it was hopeless, but I had to ask it anyway.

Tim shook his head. "The power has been taken from the

hands of the people," he said. "The power now lies with men who cannot be reached. It really isn't a democracy any more. It's a power structure of the military-industrial caste. I keep thinking of our pilots over there in Vietnam. They really don't know why they are there. They're just there because they've been ordered to go there. And I see them," Tim said quietly, holding his beer, looking out over the river, "I see them up in their planes. They've passed morning inspection. They're in freshly laundered clothes, and pressed uniforms, wearing shaving lotion, and underarm deodorant, and they're up there in those planes, dropping bombs on innocent people."

I could not speak. I turned away.

"I don't want my children growing up in such a sick society," Tim said.

Certainly no children looked less sick than Suzy and Billy. They had now been allowed to start on their picnic and they were attacking the chicken salad, each in his own little mess of potato chips, spilled orange juice, and mashed deviled eggs. Under the trees the dusk began to creep in, an enemy moving by stealth. But Kate had brought candles, the sort of candles intended to keep mosquitoes at bay, and she lighted these now to vanquish the darkness. Over the river the sky stood high and bright, still, and a breeze sprang up and suddenly ruffled the napkins.

Kate was talking with Laura as she prepared plates for us. "If there is anything you need, just write to me," she said. "I will be your agent. For things you may not be able to buy there," she said, "or for things you may have forgotten."

"That's so generous of you," Laura said, wiping Suzy's mouth, and tucking the blanket around little Matthew, where he lay in his travel basket, with his bottle. And I thought, suddenly, looking at all of them, that now I knew how Moses must have felt. I had come with them as far as I could go. I could go no farther. If a promised land lay ahead, a better land than we had known, where there would be no wars, and where people would live in harmony and equality, I would not see that. The future lay in Tim and his sons, the future of a promised land that I would never know.

We ate our picnic dinner, and when that was done, and darkness came, we gathered up all of the pieces and put it back together again in the back of the station wagon, and then we went back home. The packed Volkswagen waited in our driveway. The Bailey house had been locked, and the key turned over to the rental agent. They came into our house to wash their hands, and the faces of the children, and then they would be off on the first leg of their journey. Billy and Suzy somehow wormed their way through the length of the packed interior of the Volkswagen, to a ledge they had made for themselves on packing cases at the back window, and there they were, beaming excitedly and waving, even before the motor of the Volkswagen had been turned on. Laura fixed Matthew in his basket, and settled him behind her at the back of her seat, while she and Kate talked together in the practical tones women use to talk of practical matters in times of crisis, and Tim stopped to shake my hand before he climbed in behind the wheel.

"You are our hostage to the future," I said, grasping his hand. "There is a good part of my honor that goes with you, and you must take care of that, and bring it back to me some-day, intact."

Tim smiled in the darkness. "I will try to do that," he said, and then he got up behind the wheel. Laura was inside, and the motor turned over, and then they wheeled around in the driveway, and were out and off. In my heart of hearts I believed in everything that Tim believed, and when he had gone I wept.

In the shadows behind the trees, the dark bulk of the old house loomed, where we had lived for so many years of our life, where we had brought up a son, and from where he had gone from us, and now we were alone again, twice bereft. The process of growing older, I told myself again, was not so much a matter of giving things up as it was of having things give one up. But at least we had made a decision. We had built a new house, to stay where we had lived for so long, and we had that house, and our new life there.

We turned back to it now, where the picnic litter waited for us, to be cleaned up. As we went in the door the telephone was ringing. It was ringing with that sort of weary impatience which made me feel that it had been ringing for some time, and I hurried to pick it up. At the other end was Bert Thompson, that literary agent without peer. "Where have you been?" he said.

"We were having a picnic," I said.

"Let's not take time for jokes," Bert said. "I've been trying to get you for hours, and I want to leave the office. And I want to ask you not to say anything, not a word, until I have finished with what I have to say."

"All right," I said. I sat down on the chair beside the telephone in the hall. When Bert said things like that, I knew it was best to sit down.

"Have you ever heard of Harry Osborne?" he asked.

"No," I said. "I have never heard of Harry Osborne."

"Well, he is sort of new on the scene," Bert said, "but he is very hot just now, and I showed him the manuscript of the novel you've been working on, and he likes it. As a matter of fact, he thinks it's great."

"That's very nice," I said. "I hope you thanked him."

218

"Now I know you've had a couple of rough experiences," Bert said, "and I told Harry that, but I want you to think over very carefully what I am about to say."

"All right," I said again.

"Harry sees a musical comedy in your novel," Bert said. "He's really turned on about it. He wants to know if you would be willing to write the book for him."

I began to laugh. The only thing I knew about musical comedy was just what everyone else knew about it who had ever sat out in front of one. When Bert spoke of writing the "book" for a musical comedy I didn't even know what that meant. I wouldn't know where to begin. But I felt quite sure that I did know what Harry Osborne would be like. I could see him now in that world of his, that frantic refuge for unstable minds, surrounded by disaster, chaos, early insanity. I wanted to get mixed up in that? We had it made. The transition from our old life to a new life had not always been easy, but we were there, and I liked to think that at least we had sense enough to know when we were well off. I would deliberately leave that again for the snake pit of the theater?

"Why are you laughing?" Bert said. "What's so funny? What will I tell Harry? Will you do it?"

"I was laughing because you are always so damnably uncanny in your timing," I said. "Of course I'll do it. What have I got to lose?"

About the Author

Born in Springfield, Ohio, and educated in Ceveland, Bentz Plagemann is a former bookseller as well as a long-established writer. He is the author of nine previous books including *The Steel Cocoon, This is Goggle, Father to the Man* and *The Best Is Yet To Be,* and an autobiography, *My Place to Stand.* His most recent novel, *The Heart of Silence,* received the 1968 Ohioana Library Award for fiction. Mr. Plagemann lives with his wife in Palisades, New York.